THE TALE OF
Despereaux

Kate DiCamillo is a *New York Times* bestselling author whose books have been translated into over thirty different languages across the world. She is also a regular winner of awards, most notably the prestigious Newbery Medal, which she won for both *Flora and Ulysses: The Illuminated Adventures* and *The Tale of Despereaux*, which was made into a feature-length film in 2008. Of *The Tale of Despereaux*, Kate says, "My best friend's son asked me if I would write a story for him. 'It's about an unlikely hero,' he said, 'one with exceptionally large ears.' 'What happens to this hero?' I asked. 'I don't know,' he said. 'That's why I want you to write the story, so we can find out.'" Kate DiCamillo lives in Minneapolis, USA.

Books by the same author

Because of Winn-Dixie
The Magician's Elephant
The Miraculous Journey of Edward Tulane
Flora & Ulysses: The Illuminated Adventures
The Tiger Rising

For younger readers

Bink and Gollie
Bink and Gollie: Best Friends For Ever
Bink and Gollie: Two for One
Great Joy
Mercy Watson to the Rescue
Mercy Watson Goes for a Ride
Mercy Watson Fights Crime
Mercy Watson: Princess in Disguise
Mercy Watson Thinks Like a Pig
Mercy Watson: Something Wonky This Way Comes

THE TALE OF
Despereaux

*The story of a mouse,
a princess, some soup and
a spool of thread*

Kate DiCamillo

illustrated by Timothy Basil Ering

**WALKER
BOOKS**

*For Luke, who asked for
the story of an unlikely hero*

First published in Great Britain 2004 by Walker Books Ltd
87 Vauxhall Walk, London SE11 5HJ

This edition published 2015

4 6 8 10 9 7 5

Text © 2003 Kate DiCamillo
Illustrations © 2003 Timothy Basil Ering

The right of Kate DiCamillo and Timothy Basil Ering to be identified as
author and illustrator respectively of this work has been asserted by them
in accordance with the Copyright, Designs and Patents Act 1988

This book has been typeset in Dante

Printed and bound in Great Britain by Clays Ltd, St Ives plc

British Library Cataloguing in Publication Data:
a catalogue record for this book is available from the British Library

ISBN 978-1-4063-6852-9

www.walker.co.uk

Contents

The world is dark, and light is precious.
Come closer, dear reader.
You must trust me.
I am telling you a story.

Book
THE FIRST

*A Mouse
Is Born*

Chapter One *the last one*

THIS STORY BEGINS within the walls of a castle, with the birth of a mouse. A small mouse. The last mouse born to his parents and the only one of his litter to be born alive.

"Where are my babies?" said the exhausted mother when the ordeal was over. "Show to me my babies."

The father mouse held the one small mouse up high.

"There is only this one," he said. "The others are dead."

"*Mon Dieu*, just the one mouse baby?"

"Just the one. Will you name him?"

"All of that work for nothing," said the mother. She sighed. "It is so sad. It is such the disappointment." She was a French mouse who had arrived at the castle long ago in the luggage of a visiting French diplomat. "Disappointment" was one of her favourite words. She used it often.

"Will you name him?" repeated the father.

"Will I name him? Will I name him? Of course, I will name him, but he will only die like the others. Oh, so sad. Oh, such the tragedy."

The mouse mother held a handkerchief to her nose and then waved it in front of her face. She sniffed. "I will name him. Yes. I will name this mouse Despereaux, for all the sadness, for the many despairs in this place. Now, where is my mirror?"

Her husband handed her a small shard of mirror. The mouse mother, whose name was Antoinette, looked at her reflection and gasped aloud. "Toulèse," she said to one of her sons, "get for me my make-up bag. My eyes are a fright."

While Antoinette touched up her eye make-up, the mouse father put Despereaux down on a bed made of blanket scraps. The April sun, weak but determined, shone through a castle window and from there squeezed itself through a small hole in the wall and placed one golden finger on the little mouse.

The other, older mice children gathered around to stare at Despereaux.

"His ears are too big," said his sister Merlot. "Those are the biggest ears I've ever seen."

"Look," said a brother named Furlough, "his eyes are open. Pa, his eyes are open. They shouldn't be open."

It is true. Despereaux's eyes should not have been open. But they were. He was staring at the sun reflecting off his mother's mirror. The light was shining onto the ceiling in an oval of brilliance, and he was smiling up at the sight.

"There's something wrong with him," said the father. "Leave him alone."

Despereaux's brothers and sisters stepped back, away from the new mouse.

"This is the last," proclaimed Antoinette from her bed. "I will have no more mice babies. They are such the disappointment. They are hard on my beauty.

Despereaux's eyes should not have been open.

They ruin, for me, my looks. This is the last one. No more."

"The last one," said the father. "And he'll be dead soon. He can't live. Not with his eyes open like that."

But, reader, he did live.

This is his story.

Chapter Two
such a disappointment

DESPEREAUX TILLING LIVED.

But his existence was cause for much speculation in the mouse community.

"He's the smallest mouse I've ever seen," said his aunt Florence. "It's ridiculous. No mouse has ever, ever been this small. Not even a Tilling." She looked at Despereaux through narrowed eyes as if she expected him to disappear entirely. "No mouse," she said again. "Ever."

Despereaux, his tail wrapped around his feet, stared back at her.

"Those are some big ears he's got, too," observed

his uncle Alfred. "They look more like donkey ears, if you ask me."

"They are obscenely large ears," said Aunt Florence.

Despereaux wiggled his ears.

His aunt Florence gasped.

"They say he was born with his eyes open," whispered Uncle Alfred.

Despereaux stared hard at his uncle.

"Impossible," said Aunt Florence. "No mouse, no matter how small or obscenely large-eared, is ever born with his eyes open. It simply isn't done."

"His pa, Lester, says he's not well," said Uncle Alfred.

Despereaux sneezed.

He said nothing in defence of himself. How could he? Everything his aunt and uncle said was true. He *was* ridiculously small. His ears *were* obscenely large. He *had* been born with his eyes open. And he was sickly. He coughed and sneezed so often that he carried a handkerchief in one paw at all times. He ran temperatures. He fainted at loud noises. Most alarming of all, he showed no interest in the things a mouse should show interest in.

He did not think constantly of food. He was not intent on tracking down every crumb. While his larger, older siblings ate, Despereaux stood with his head cocked to one side, holding very still.

"Do you hear that sweet, sweet sound?" he said.

"I hear the sound of cake crumbs falling out of people's mouths and hitting the floor," said his brother Toulèse. "That's what I hear."

"No…" said Despereaux. "It's something else. It sounds like … um … honey."

"You might have big ears," said Toulèse, "but they're not attached right to your brain. You don't *hear* honey. You *smell* honey. When there's honey to smell. Which there isn't."

"Son!" barked Despereaux's father. "Snap to it. Get your head out of the clouds and hunt for crumbs."

"Please," said his mother, "look for the crumbs. Eat them to make your mama happy. You are such the skinny mouse. You are a disappointment to your mama."

"Sorry," said Despereaux. He lowered his head and sniffed the castle floor.

But, reader, he was not smelling.

He was listening, with his big ears, to the sweet sound that no other mouse seemed to hear.

Chapter Three
once upon a time

DESPEREAUX'S SIBLINGS tried to educate him in the ways of being a mouse. His brother Furlough took him on a tour of the castle to demonstrate the art of scurrying.

"Move from side to side," instructed Furlough, scrabbling across the waxed castle floor. "Look over your shoulder all the time, first to the right, then to the left. Don't stop for anything."

But Despereaux wasn't listening to Furlough. He was staring at the light pouring in through the stained-glass windows of the castle. He stood on his hind legs and held his handkerchief over his heart and stared up, up, up into the brilliant light.

"Furlough," he said, "what is this thing? What are all these colours? Are we in heaven?"

"Cripes!" shouted Furlough from a far corner. "Don't stand there in the middle of the floor talking about heaven. Move! You're a mouse, not a man. You've got to scurry."

"What?" said Despereaux, still staring at the light.

But Furlough was gone.

He had, like a good mouse, disappeared into a hole in the moulding.

Despereaux's sister Merlot took him into the castle library, where light came streaming in through tall, high windows and landed on the floor in bright yellow patches.

"Here," said Merlot, "follow me, small brother, and I will instruct you on the fine points of how to nibble paper."

Merlot scurried up a chair and from there hopped onto a table on which there sat a huge, open book.

"This way, small brother," she said as she crawled

onto the pages of the book.

And Despereaux followed her from the chair, to the table, to the page.

"Now then," said Merlot. "This glue, here, is tasty, and the paper edges are crunchy and yummy, like so." She nibbled the edge of a page and then looked over at Despereaux.

"You try," she said. "First a bite of some glue and then follow it with a crunch of the paper. And these squiggles, they are very tasty."

Despereaux looked down at the book, and something remarkable happened. The marks on the pages, the "squiggles" as Merlot called them, arranged themselves into shapes. The shapes arranged themselves into words, and the words spelled out a delicious and wonderful phrase: *Once upon a time*.

"'Once upon a time,'" whispered Despereaux.

"What?" said Merlot.

"Nothing."

"Eat," said Merlot.

"I couldn't possibly," said Despereaux, backing away from the book.

"'Once upon a time,'" whispered Despereaux.

"Why?"

"Um," said Despereaux, "it would ruin the story."

"The story? What story?" Merlot stared at him. A piece of paper trembled at the end of one of her indignant whiskers. "It's just like Pa said when you were born. Something is not right with you." She turned and scurried from the library to tell her parents about this latest disappointment.

Despereaux waited until she was gone, and then he reached out and, with one paw, touched the lovely words. *Once upon a time.*

He shivered. He sneezed. He blew his nose into his handkerchief.

"'Once upon a time,'" he said aloud, relishing the sound. And then, tracing each word with his paw, he read the story of a beautiful princess and the brave knight who serves and honours her.

Despereaux did not know it, but he would need, very soon, to be brave himself.

Have I mentioned that beneath the castle there was a dungeon? In the dungeon, there were rats. Large rats. Mean rats.

Despereaux was destined to meet those rats.

Reader, you must know that an interesting fate (sometimes involving rats, sometimes not) awaits almost everyone, mouse or man, who does not conform.

Chapter Four
enter the Pea

DESPEREAUX'S BROTHERS AND SISTERS soon abandoned the thankless task of trying to educate him in the ways of being a mouse.

And so Despereaux was free.

He spent his days as he wanted: He wandered through the rooms of the castle, staring dreamily at the light streaming in through the stained-glass windows. He went to the library and read over and over again the story of the fair maiden and the knight who rescued her. And he discovered, finally, the source of the honey-sweet sound.

The sound was music.

The sound was King Phillip playing his guitar and singing to his daughter, the Princess Pea, every night before she fell asleep.

Hidden in a hole in the wall of the princess's bedroom, the mouse listened with all his heart. The sound of the king's music made Despereaux's soul grow large and light inside of him.

"Oh," he said, "it sounds like heaven. It smells like honey."

He stuck his left ear out of the hole in the wall so that he could hear the music better, and then he stuck his right ear out so that he could hear better still. And it wasn't too long before one of his paws followed his head and then another paw, and then, without any real planning on Despereaux's part, the whole of him was on display, all in an effort to get closer to the music.

Now, while Despereaux did not indulge in much of the normal behaviour of mice, he did adhere to one of the most basic and elemental of all mice rules: Do not ever, under any circumstances, reveal yourself to humans.

But ... the music, the music. The music made him

lose his head and act against the few small mouse instincts he was in possession of, and because of this he revealed himself; and in no time at all, he was spied by the sharp-eyed Princess Pea.

"Oh, Papa," she said. "Look, a mouse."

The king stopped singing. He squinted. The king was near-sighted; that is, anything that was not right in front of his eyes was very difficult for him to see.

"Where?" said the king.

"There," said the Princess Pea. She pointed.

"That, my dear Pea, is a bug, not a mouse. It is much too small to be a mouse."

"No, no, it's a mouse."

"A bug," said the king, who liked to be right.

"A *mouse*," said the Pea, who knew that she was right.

As for Despereaux, he was beginning to realize that he had made a very grave error. He trembled. He shook. He sneezed. He considered fainting.

"He's frightened," said the Pea. "Look, he's so afraid he's shaking. I think he was listening to the music. Play something, Papa."

"A king play music for a *bug*?" King Phillip wrinkled his forehead. "Is that proper, do you think? Wouldn't that make this into some kind of topsy-turvy, wrong-headed world if a king played music for a bug?"

"Papa, I told you, he's a *mouse*," said the Pea. "Please?"

"Oh, well, if it will make you happy, I, the king, will play music for a bug."

"A *mouse*," corrected the Pea.

The king adjusted his heavy gold crown. He cleared his throat. He strummed the guitar and started to sing a song about stardust. The song was as sweet as light shining through stained-glass windows, as captivating as the story in a book.

Despereaux forgot all his fear. He only wanted to hear the music.

He crept closer and then closer still, until, reader, he was sitting right at the foot of the king.

Chapter Five
what Furlough saw

THE PRINCESS PEA looked down at Despereaux. She smiled at him. And while her father played another song, a song about the deep purple falling over sleepy garden walls, the princess reached out and touched the top of the mouse's head.

Despereaux stared up at her in wonder. The Pea, he decided, looked just like the picture of the fair maiden in the book in the library. The princess smiled at Despereaux again, and this time, Despereaux smiled back. And then, something incredible happened: The mouse fell in love.

Reader, you may ask this question; in fact, you

Despereaux stared up at her in wonder.

must ask this question: Is it ridiculous for a very small, sickly, big-eared mouse to fall in love with a beautiful human princess named Pea?

The answer is … yes. Of course, it's ridiculous.

Love is ridiculous.

But love is also wonderful. And powerful. And Despereaux's love for the Princess Pea would prove, in time, to be all of these things: powerful, wonderful and ridiculous.

"You're so sweet," said the princess to Despereaux. "You're so tiny."

As Despereaux looked up at her adoringly, Furlough happened to scurry past the princess's room, moving his head left to right, right to left, back and forth.

"Cripes!" said Furlough. He stopped. He stared into the princess's room. His whiskers became as tight as bowstrings.

What Furlough saw was Despereaux Tilling sitting at the foot of the king. What Furlough saw was the princess touching the top of his brother's head.

"Cripes!" shouted Furlough again. "Oh, cripes! He's nuts! He's a goner!"

And, executing a classic scurry, Furlough went off to tell his father, Lester Tilling, the terrible, unbelievable news of what he had just seen.

Chapter Six
this drum

"HE CANNOT, he simply cannot be my son," Lester said. He clutched his whiskers with his front paws and shook his head from side to side in despair.

"Of course he is your son," said Antoinette. "What do you mean he is not your son? This is a ridiculous statement. Why must you always make the ridiculous statements?"

"You," said Lester. "This is your fault. The French blood in him has made him crazy."

"C'est moi?" said Antoinette. *"C'est moi?* Why must it always be I who takes the blame? If your son

is such the disappointment, it is as much your fault as mine."

"Something must be done," said Lester. He pulled on a whisker so hard that it came loose. He waved the whisker over his head. He pointed it at his wife. "He will be the end of us all," he shouted, "sitting at the foot of a human king. Unbelievable! Unthinkable!"

"Oh, so dramatic," said Antoinette. She held out one paw and studied her painted nails. "He is a small mouse. How much of the harm can he do?"

"If there is one thing I have learnt in this world," said Lester, "it is that mice must act like mice or else there is bound to be trouble. I will call a special meeting of the Mouse Council. Together, we will decide what must be done."

"Oh," said Antoinette, "you and this council of the mouse. It is a waste of the time in my opinion."

"Don't you understand?" shouted Lester. "He must be punished. He must be brought up before the tribunal." He pushed past her and dug furiously through a pile of paper scraps, until he uncovered a thimble with a piece of leather stretched across its open end.

"Oh, please," said Antoinette. She covered her ears. "Not this drum of the council of the mouse."

"Yes," said Lester, "the drum." He held it up high above his head, first to the north and then to the south, and then to the east and the west. He lowered it and turned his back to his wife and closed his eyes and took a deep breath and began to beat the drum slowly, one long beat with his tail, two staccato beats with his paws.

Boom. Tat-tat. Boom. Tat-tat. Boom. Tat-tat.

The rhythm of the drum was a signal for the members of the Mouse Council.

Boom. Tat-tat. Boom. Tat-tat. Boom.

The beating of the drum let them know that an important decision would have to be made, one that affected the safety and wellbeing of the entire mouse community.

Boom. Tat-tat. Boom. Tat-tat.
Boom.

Chapter Seven
a mouse in love

AND WHAT WAS OUR OWN favourite member of the mouse community doing while the sound of the Mouse Council drum echoed through the walls of the castle?

Reader, I must report that Furlough had not seen the worst of it. Despereaux sat with the princess and the king and listened to song after song. At one point, gently, oh so gently, the Pea picked up the mouse in her hand. She cupped him in her palm and scratched his oversized ears.

"You have lovely ears," the Pea said to him. "They are like small pieces of velvet."

Despereaux thought that he might faint with the pleasure of someone referring to his ears as small and lovely. He laid his tail against the Pea's wrist to steady himself and he felt the princess's pulse, the pounding of her heart, and his own heart immediately took up the rhythm of hers.

"Papa," the Pea said when the music was over, "I am going to keep this mouse. We are going to be great friends."

The king looked at Despereaux cupped in his daughter's hands. He narrowed his eyes. "A mouse," he muttered. "A *rodent*."

"What?" said the Pea.

"Put it down," the king commanded.

"No," said the Pea, who was a person not at all used to being told what to do. "I mean, why should I?"

"Because I told you to."

"But why?" protested the Pea.

"Because it's a mouse."

"I know. I'm the one who told you he was a mouse."

"I wasn't thinking," said the king.

"Thinking of what?"

"Your mother. The queen."

"My mother," said the Pea sadly.

"Mice are rodents," said the king. He adjusted his crown. "They are related to ... rats. You know how we feel about rats. You know of our own dark history with rats."

The Pea shuddered.

"But Papa," she said, "he is not a rat. He's a mouse. There's a difference."

"Royalty," the king said, "has many responsibilities. And one of them is not getting personally involved with even the distant relatives of one's enemies. Put him down, Pea."

The princess put Despereaux down.

"Good girl," said the king. And then he looked at Despereaux. "Scat," he said.

Despereaux, however, did not scat. He sat and stared up at the princess.

The king stamped his foot. "Scat!" he shouted.

"Papa," said the princess, "please, don't be mean to him." And she began to weep.

Despereaux, seeing her tears, broke the last of the

great, ancient rules of mice. He spoke. To a human.

"Please," said Despereaux, "don't cry." He held out his handkerchief to the princess.

The Pea sniffed and leaned down close to him.

"Do not speak to her!" thundered the king.

Despereaux dropped his handkerchief. He backed away from the king.

"Rodents do not speak to princesses. We will not have this becoming a topsy-turvy, wrong-headed world. There are rules. Scat. Get lost, before my common sense returns and I have you killed."

The king stamped his foot again. Despereaux found it alarming to have such a big foot brought down with so much force and anger so close to his own small head. He ran towards the hole in the wall.

But he turned before he entered it. He turned and shouted to the princess, "My name is Despereaux!"

"Despereaux?" she said.

"I honour you!" shouted Despereaux.

"I honour you" was what the knight said to the fair maiden in the story that Despereaux read every day in the book in the library. Despereaux had muttered the phrase often to himself, but he had never before this evening had occasion to use it when speaking to someone else.

"Get out of here!" shouted the king, stamping his foot harder and then harder still so it seemed as if the whole castle, the very world, were shaking. "Rodents know nothing of honour."

Despereaux ran into the hole and from there he looked out at the princess. She had picked up his handkerchief and she was looking at him ... right, directly into his soul.

"Despereaux," she said. He saw his name on her lips.

"I honour you," whispered Despereaux. "I honour you." He put his paw over his heart. He bowed so low that his whiskers touched the floor.

He was, alas, a mouse deeply in love.

Chapter Eight
to the rats

THE REST OF THE MOUSE COUNCIL, twelve honoured mice and one Most Very Honoured Head Mouse, heeded the call of Lester's drum and gathered in a small, secret hole off King Phillip's throne room. The thirteen mice sat around a piece of wood balanced on spools of thread and listened in horror while Despereaux's father related the story of what Furlough had seen.

"At the foot of the king," said Lester.

"Her finger right on top of his head," said Lester.

"He was looking up at her, and … it was not in fear."

The Mouse Council members listened with their mouths open. They listened with their whiskers drooping and their ears flat against their heads. They listened in dismay and outrage and fear.

When Lester finished, there was a silence dismal and deep.

"Something," intoned the Most Very Honoured Head Mouse, "is wrong with your son. He is not well. This goes beyond his fevers, beyond his large ears and his lack of growth. He is deeply disturbed. His behaviour endangers us all. Humans cannot be trusted. We know this to be an indisputable fact. A mouse who consorts with humans, a mouse who would sit right at the foot of a man, *a mouse who would allow a human to touch him*" – and here, the entire Mouse Council indulged in a collective shiver of disgust – "cannot be trusted. That is the way of the world, our world.

"Fellow mice, it is my most fervent hope that Despereaux has not spoken to these humans. But obviously, we can assume nothing. And this is a time to act, not wonder."

Lester nodded his head in agreement. And the

twelve other members of the Mouse Council nodded their heads too.

"We have no choice," said the Head Mouse. "He must go to the dungeon." He pounded his fisted paw on the table. "He must go to the rats. Immediately. Members of the council, I will now ask you to vote. Those in favour of Despereaux being sent to the dungeon, say 'aye'."

There was a chorus of sad "ayes".

"Those opposed say 'nay'."

Silence reigned in the room.

The only noise came from Lester. He was crying.

And thirteen mice, ashamed for Lester, looked away.

Reader, can you imagine your own father not voting against your being sent to a dungeon full of rats? Can you imagine him not saying one word in your defence?

Despereaux's father wept and the Most Very Honoured Head Mouse beat his paw against the table again and said, "Despereaux Tilling will appear before the mouse community. He will hear of his sins; he will be given a chance to deny them.

If he does not deny them, he will be allowed to renounce them so that he may go to the dungeon with a pure heart. Despereaux Tilling is hereby called to sit with the Mouse Council."

At least Lester had the decency to weep at his act of perfidy. Reader, do you know what "perfidy" means? I have a feeling you do, based on the little scene that has just unfolded here. But you should look up the word in your dictionary, just to be sure.

Chapter Nine
the right question

THE MOUSE COUNCIL sent Furlough to collect Despereaux. And Furlough found his brother in the library, standing on top of the great, open book, his tail wrapped tightly around his feet, his small body shivering.

Despereaux was reading the story out loud to himself. He was reading from the beginning so that he could get to the end, where the reader was assured that the knight and the fair maiden lived together happily ever after.

Despereaux wanted to read those words: *Happily ever after*. He needed to say them aloud; he needed some assurance that this feeling he had for the Princess Pea, this love, would come to a good end. And so he was reading the story as if it were a spell and as if the words of it, spoken aloud, could make magic happen.

"See here," said Furlough out loud to himself. He looked at his brother and then looked away. "This is just the kind of thing I'm talking about. This is exactly the kind of thing. What's he doing here, for cripes' sake? He's not eating the paper. He's *talking* to the paper. It's wrong, wrong, wrong."

"Hey," he said to Despereaux.

Despereaux kept reading.

"Hey!" shouted Furlough. "Despereaux! The Mouse Council wants you."

"Pardon?" said Despereaux. He looked up from the book.

"The Mouse Council has called you to sit with them."

"Me?" said Despereaux.

"You."

"I'm busy right now," said Despereaux, and he bent his head again to the open book.

Furlough sighed. "Geez," he said. "Cripes. Nothing makes sense to this guy. Nothing. I was right to turn him in. He's sick."

Furlough crawled up the chair leg and then hopped onto the book. He sat next to Despereaux. He tapped him on the head once, twice.

"Hey," he said. "The Mouse Council isn't asking. They're telling. They're *commanding*. You have to come with me. Right now."

Despereaux turned to him. "Do you know what love is?" he said.

"Huh?"

"Love."

Furlough shook his head. "You're asking the wrong question," he said. "The question you should be asking is why the Mouse Council wants to see you."

"There is somebody who loves me," said Despereaux. "And I love her and that is the only thing that matters to me."

"Somebody who loves you? Somebody who you love? What difference does that make? What matters is that you're in a lot of trouble with the Mouse Council."

"Her name," said Despereaux, "is Pea."

"What?"

"The person who loves me. Her name is Pea."

"Cripes," said Furlough, "you're missing the whole point of everything here. You're missing the point of being a mouse. You're missing the point of being called to sit with the Mouse Council. You've got to come with me. It's the law. You've been called."

Despereaux sighed. He reached out and touched the words *fair maiden* in the book. He traced them with one paw. And then he put his paw to his mouth.

"Cripes," said Furlough. "You're making a fool of yourself. Let's go."

"I honour you," whispered Despereaux. "I honour you."

And then, reader, he followed Furlough over the book and down the chair leg and across the library floor to the waiting Mouse Council.

He allowed his brother to lead him to his fate.

Chapter Ten
good reasons

THE ENTIRE MOUSE COMMUNITY, as instructed by the Most Very Honoured Head Mouse, had gathered behind the wall of the castle ballroom. The members of the Mouse Council sat atop three bricks piled high, and spread out before them was every mouse, old and young, foolish and wise, who lived in the castle.

They were all waiting for Despereaux.

"Make way," said Furlough. "Here he is. I've got him. Make way."

Furlough pushed through the crowd of mice. Despereaux clung to his brother's tail.

"There he is," the mice whispered. "There he is."

"He's so small."

"They say he was born with his eyes open."

Some of the mice pulled away from Despereaux in disgust, and others, thrill-seekers, reached out to touch him with a whisker or a paw.

"The princess put a finger on him."

"They say he sat at the foot of the king."

"It is simply not done!" came the distinctive voice of Despereaux's aunt Florence.

"Make way, make way!" shouted Furlough. "I have him right here. I have Despereaux Tilling, who has been called to sit with the Mouse Council."

He led Despereaux to the front of the room. "Honoured members of the Mouse Council," shouted Furlough, "I have brought you Despereaux Tilling, as you requested, to sit with you." He looked over his shoulder at Despereaux. "Let go of me," Furlough said.

Despereaux dropped Furlough's tail. He looked up at the members of the Mouse Council. His father met his gaze and then shook his head and looked away. Despereaux turned and faced the sea of mice.

"To the dungeon!" a voice cried out. "Straight to the dungeon with him."

Despereaux's head, which had been full of such delightful phrases as "happily ever after" and "lovely ears" and "I honour you", suddenly cleared.

"Straight to the dungeon!" another voice shouted.

"Enough," said the Most Very Honoured Head Mouse. "This trial will be conducted in an orderly fashion. We will act civilized." He cleared his throat. He said to Despereaux, "Son, turn and look at me."

Despereaux turned. He looked up and into the Head Mouse's eyes. They were dark eyes, deep and sad and frightened. And as Despereaux looked into them, his heart thudded once, twice.

"Despereaux Tilling," said the Head Mouse.

"Yes, sir," said Despereaux.

"We, the fourteen members of the Mouse Council, have discussed your behaviour. First, we will give you a chance to defend yourself against these rumours of your egregious acts. Did you or did you not sit at the foot of the human king?"

"I did," said Despereaux, "but I was listening to

the music, sir. I was there to hear the song that the king was singing."

"To hear the what?"

"The song, sir. He was singing a song about the deep purple falling over sleepy garden walls."

The Head Mouse shook his head. "Whatever you are talking about is beside the point. The question is this and only this: Did you sit at the foot of the human king?"

"I did, sir."

The community of mice shifted their tails and paws and whiskers. They waited.

"And did you allow the girl human, the princess, to touch you?"

"Her name is Pea."

"Never mind her name. Did you allow her to touch you?"

"Yes, sir," said Despereaux. "I let her touch me. It felt good."

A gasp arose from the assembled mice.

Despereaux heard his mother's voice. *"Mon Dieu,* it is not the end of the world. It was a touch, what of it?"

"It is simply not done!" came Aunt Florence's voice from the crowd.

"To the dungeon," said a mouse in the front row.

"Silence!" roared the Most Very Honoured Head Mouse. "Silence." He looked down at Despereaux.

"Do you, Despereaux Tilling, understand the sacred, never-to-be-broken rules of conduct for being a mouse?"

"Yes, sir," said Despereaux, "I guess so. But…"

"Did you break them?"

"Yes, sir," said Despereaux. He raised his voice. "But … I broke the rules for good reasons. Because of music. And because of love."

"Love!" said the Head Mouse.

"Oh, cripes," said Furlough, "here we go."

"I love her, sir," said Despereaux.

"We are not here to talk about love. This trial is not about love. This trial is about you being a mouse," shouted the Most Very Honoured Head Mouse from high atop the bricks, "and *not acting like one!!!*"

"Yes, sir," said Despereaux. "I know."

"No, I don't think that you do know. And because you do not deny the charges, you must be punished.

You are to be sent, as ancient castle-mouse law decrees, to the dungeon. You are being sent to the rats."

"That's right!" called out a mouse in the crowd. "That's the ticket."

The dungeon! The rats! Despereaux's small heart sank all the way to the tip of his tail. There would be no light in the dungeon. No stained-glass windows. No library and no books. There would be no Princess Pea.

"But first," said the Most Very Honoured Head Mouse, "we will give you the chance to renounce your actions. We will allow you to go to the dungeon with a pure heart."

"Renounce?"

"Repent. Say that you are sorry you sat at the foot of the human king. Say that you are sorry you allowed the human princess to touch you. Say that you regret these actions."

Despereaux felt hot and then cold and then hot again. Renounce her? Renounce the princess?

"Mon Dieu!" shouted his mother. "Son, do not act the fool. Renounce! Repent!"

"What say you, Despereaux Tilling?"

"I say ... I say ... I say ... *no*," whispered Despereaux.

"What?" said the Head Mouse.

"No," said Despereaux. And this time, he did not whisper the word. "I am not sorry. I will not renounce my actions. I love her. I love the princess."

There was a bellow of collective outrage. The whole of the mouse community surged toward Despereaux. The mice seemed to become one angry body with hundreds of tails and thousands of whiskers and one huge, hungry mouth opening and closing and opening and closing, saying over and over and over again, "To the dungeon. To the dungeon. To the dungeon."

The words pounded through Despereaux's body with each beat of his heart.

"Very well," said the Most Very Honoured Head Mouse. "You will die, then, with a black heart. Threadmaster," he called, "bring out the thread."

Despereaux marvelled at his own bravery.

He admired his own defiance.

And then, reader, he fainted.

Chapter Eleven
the threadmaster cometh

WHEN DESPEREAUX CAME TO, he heard the drum. His father was beating a rhythm that had much more *boom* and much less *tat*. Together, Lester and the drum produced an ominous sound that went something like this: *Boom-boom-boom-tat. Boom-boom-boom-tat.*

"Make way for the thread!" cried a mouse who was pushing a wooden spool of red thread through the crowd. "Make way for the thread!"

Boom-boom-boom-tat, went the drum.

"To the dungeon!" shouted the mice.

Despereaux lay on his back, blinking his eyes.

How, he wondered, had things gone so terribly wrong? Wasn't it a good thing, to love? In the story in the book, love was a very good thing. Because the knight loved the fair maiden, he was able to rescue her. They lived happily ever after. It said so. In the book. They were the last words on the page. *Happily ever after.* Despereaux was certain that he had read exactly those words time and time again.

Lying on the floor with the drum beating and the mice shouting and the threadmaster calling out, "Make way, make way," Despereaux had a sudden, chilling thought: had some other mouse eaten the words that spoke the truth? Did the knight and the fair maiden actually *not* live happily ever after?

Reader, do you believe that there is such a thing as happily ever after? Or, like Despereaux, have you, too, begun to question the possibility of happy endings?

"Happily ever after," whispered Despereaux. "Happily ever after," he said again as the spool of thread came to a stop beside him.

"The thread, the thread, the thread," murmured the mice.

"I'm sorry," said the mouse behind the spool, "but

I have to ask you to stand up. I have to do my job."

Despereaux got slowly to his feet.

"On your hind legs, please," said the threadmaster. "It's the rules."

Despereaux stood on his hind legs.

"Thank you," said the mouse. "I appreciate it."

While Despereaux watched, the threadmaster unwound a length of red thread from the spool and tied a loop.

"Just enough for the neck," muttered the mouse. "No more, no less. That's what the last threadmaster taught me: enough thread for the neck." He looked up at Despereaux and then back down at the loop of thread. "And you, my friend, have a small neck."

The threadmaster raised his arms and put them around Despereaux's neck. He leant in close and Despereaux smelt celery. He could feel the threadmaster's breath in his ear as he worked at tightening the thread.

"Is she beautiful?" the threadmaster whispered.

"What?" said Despereaux.

"Shhhh. Is the princess beautiful?"

"The Princess Pea?"

*"Just enough for the neck," muttered the mouse.
"No more, no less."*

"Yes."

"She is lovely beyond all imagining," said Despereaux.

"Just right," the threadmaster said. He drew back. He nodded his head. "A lovely princess, just so, like a fairy tale. And you love her, as a knight loves a maiden. You love her with a courtly love, a love that is based on bravery and courtesy and honour and devotion. Just so."

"How do you know that?" Despereaux said. "How do you know about fairy tales?"

"Shhhhh." The mouse leant in close, and Despereaux smelt celery again, green and alive. "Be brave, friend," whispered the threadmaster. "Be brave for the princess." And then he stepped back and turned and shouted, "Fellow mice, the thread has been tied. The thread has been knotted."

A roar of approval went up from the crowd.

Despereaux squared his shoulders. He had made a decision. He would do as the threadmaster had suggested. He would be brave for the princess.

Even if (reader, could it be true?) there was no such thing as happily ever after.

Chapter Twelve
adieu

THE SOUND OF THE DRUM changed again. The final *tat* disappeared and it became nothing but *boom*.

Boom, boom, boom.

Boom, boom, boom.

Lester used only his tail, bringing it down with great force and seriousness upon the drum.

The threadmaster retreated.

The room full of mice fell silent, expectant, waiting.

And as Despereaux stood before them with the red thread around his neck and the fourteen members of the Mouse Council perched on the bricks above him, two burly mice came forward. Black pieces of cloth covered their heads. There were slits for their eyes.

"We," said the bigger of the two mice, "will escort you to the dungeon."

"Despereaux," Antoinette called out. "Ah, my Despereaux!"

Despereaux looked out into the crowd of mice and saw his mother. She was easy to spot. In honour of her youngest mouse being sent to the dungeon, she had put on a tremendous amount of make-up.

The hooded mice each put a paw on one of Despereaux's shoulders.

"It's time," said the one on the left, the first hood.

Antoinette pushed her way through the crowd. "He is my son," she said. "I want to have a last word with my son."

Despereaux looked at his mother. He concentrated on standing before her without trembling. He concentrated on not being a disappointment.

"Please," said Antoinette, "what will happen to him? What will happen to my baby?"

"Ma'am," said the first hood. His voice was deep and slow. "You don't want to know."

"I want to know. I want to know. He is my child. The child of my heart. The last of my mice babies."

The hooded mice said nothing.

"Tell me," said Antoinette.

"The rats," said the first.

"The rats," said the second.

"Yes. Yes. *Oui*. The rats. What of them?"

"The rats will eat him," said the second hood.

"Ah," said Antoinette. *"Mon Dieu!"*

At the thought of being eaten by rats, Despereaux forgot about being brave. He forgot about not being a disappointment. He felt himself heading into another faint. But his mother, who had an excellent sense of dramatic timing, beat him to it; she executed a beautiful, flawless swoon, landing right at Despereaux's feet.

"Now you've done it," said the first hood.

"It doesn't matter," said the second. "Step over her. We have a job to do. Nobody's mother is going to stop us. To the dungeon."

"To the dungeon," repeated the first hood, but

his voice, so deep and certain a moment ago, now shook a tiny bit. He put a paw on Despereaux and tugged him forwards, and the two hoods and Despereaux stepped over Antoinette.

The crowd parted.

The mice began again to chant: "To the dungeon. To the dungeon. To the dungeon."

The drumbeat continued.

Boom, boom, boom. Boom, boom, boom.

And Despereaux was led away.

At the last moment, Antoinette came out of her faint and shouted one word to her child.

That word, reader, was *adieu*.

Do you know the definition of *adieu*? Don't bother with your dictionary. I will tell you.

Adieu is the French word for farewell.

"Farewell" is not the word that you would like to hear from your mother as you are being led to the dungeon by two oversized mice in black hoods.

Words that you *would* like to hear are: "Take me instead. I will go to the dungeon in my son's place." There is a great deal of comfort in those words.

But, reader, there is no comfort in the word

"farewell", even if you say it in French. "Farewell" is a word that, in any language, is full of sorrow. It is a word that promises absolutely nothing.

Chapter Thirteen ⌒
perfidy unlimited

TOGETHER, THE THREE MICE travelled down, down, down.

The thread around Despereaux's neck was tight. He felt as if it was choking him. He tugged at it with one paw.

"Don't touch the thread," barked the second hood.

"Yeah," echoed the first hood, "don't touch the thread."

They moved quickly. And whenever Despereaux slowed down, one of the two hoods poked him in the shoulder and told him to keep moving. They went through holes in the wall and down golden stairs. They went past rooms with doors that were closed and doors that were flung wide. The three mice travelled across marble floors and under heavy velvet drapes. They moved through warm patches of sunlight and dark pools of shade.

This, thought Despereaux, was the world he was leaving behind, the world that he knew and loved. And somewhere in it, the Princess Pea was laughing and smiling and clapping her hands to music, unaware of Despereaux's fate. That he would not be able to let the princess know what had become of him seemed suddenly unbearable to the mouse.

"Would it be possible for me to have a last word with the princess?" Despereaux asked.

"A word?" said the second hood. "You want a word with a human?"

"I want to tell her what has happened to me."

"Geez," said the first hood. He stopped and stamped a paw on the floor in frustration. "Cripes. You can't learn, can you."

The voice was terribly familiar to Despereaux.

"Furlough?" he said.

"What?" said the first hood irritably.

Despereaux shuddered. His own brother was delivering him to the dungeon. His heart stopped beating and shrunk to a small, cold, disbelieving pebble. But then, just as quickly, it leapt alive again, beating with hope.

"Furlough," Despereaux said, and he took one of his brother's paws in his own. "Please, let me go. Please. I'm your brother."

Furlough rolled his eyes. He took his paw out of Despereaux's. "No," he said. "No way."

"Please," said Despereaux.

"No," said Furlough. "Rules are rules."

Reader, do you recall the word "perfidy"? As our story progresses, "perfidy" becomes an ever more appropriate word, doesn't it?

"Perfidy" was certainly the word that was in Despereaux's mind as the mice finally approached the narrow, steep stairs that led to the black hole of the dungeon.

They stood, the three mice, two with hoods and one without, and contemplated the abyss before them.

Despereaux shuddered. His own brother was delivering him to the dungeon.

And then Furlough stood up on his hind legs and placed his right paw over his heart. "For the good of the castle mice," he announced to the darkness, "we deliver this day to the dungeon, a mouse in need of punishment. He is, according to the laws we have established, wearing the red thread of death."

"The red thread of death?" repeated Despereaux in a small voice. "Wearing the red thread of death" was a terrible phrase, but the mouse didn't have long to consider its implications, because he was suddenly pushed from behind by the hooded mice.

The push was a strong one, and it sent Despereaux flying down the stairs into the dungeon. As he tumbled, whisker over tail, through the darkness, there were only two words in his mind. One was "perfidy". And the other word that he clung to was "Pea".

Perfidy. Pea. Perfidy. Pea. These were the words that pinwheeled through Despereaux's mind as his body descended into the darkness.

Chapter Fourteen
darkness

DESPEREAUX LAY ON HIS BACK at the bottom of the steps and touched the bones in his body one by one. They were all there. And, amazingly, they were unbroken. He got to his feet and became aware of a terrible, foul, extremely insulting smell.

The dungeon, reader, stank. It stank of despair and suffering and hopelessness. Which is to say that the dungeon smelled of rats.

And it was so dark. Despereaux had never before encountered darkness so awful, so all-encompassing. The darkness had a physical presence as if it were a being all of its own. The mouse held one small paw up in front of his whiskers. He could not see it, and he had the truly alarming thought that perhaps he, Despereaux Tilling, did not even exist.

"Oh my!" he said out loud.

His voice echoed in the smelly darkness.

"Perfidy," said Despereaux, just to hear his voice again, just to assure himself that he did exist.

"Pea," said Despereaux, and the name of his beloved was immediately swallowed up by the darkness.

He shivered. He shook. He sneezed. His teeth chattered. He longed for his handkerchief. He grabbed hold of his tail (it took him a long, frightening moment to even locate his tail, so absolute was the darkness) to have something, anything, to hold onto. He considered fainting. He deemed it the only reasonable response to the situation in which he found himself, but then he remembered the words of the threadmaster: honour, courtesy, devotion and bravery.

I will be brave, thought Despereaux. I will try to

be brave like a knight in shining armour. I will be brave for the Princess Pea.

How best for him to be brave?

He cleared his throat. He let go of his tail. He stood up straighter. "Once upon a time," he said out loud to the darkness. He said these words because they were the best, the most powerful words that he knew and just the saying of them comforted him.

"Once upon a time," he said again, feeling a tiny bit braver. "There was a knight and he wore, always, an armour of shining silver."

"Once upon a time?" boomed a voice from the darkness. "A knight in shining armour? What does a mouse know of such things?"

That voice, the loudest voice that Despereaux had ever heard, could only, he assumed, belong to the world's largest rat.

Despereaux's small, overworked heart stopped beating.

And for the second time that day, the mouse fainted.

Chapter Fifteen
light

WHEN DESPEREAUX AWOKE, he was cupped in the large, calloused hand of a human and he was staring into the fire of one match, and beyond the match there was a large, dark eye looking directly at him.

"A mouse with red thread," boomed the voice. "Oh, yes, Gregory knows the way of mice and rats. Gregory knows. And Gregory has his own thread, marking him. See here, mouse." And the match was held to a candle and the candle sputtered to life and Despereaux saw that there was a rope tied around the man's ankle. "Here is the difference between us:

Gregory's rope saves him. And your thread will be the death of you." The man blew the candle out and the darkness descended and the man's hand closed more tightly around Despereaux and Despereaux felt his beleaguered heart start up a crazy rhythm of fear.

"Who are you?" he whispered.

"The answer to that question, mouse, is Gregory. You are talking to Gregory the jailer, who has been buried here, keeping watch over this dungeon for decades, for centuries, for aeons. For eternities. You are talking to Gregory the jailer, who, in the richest of ironies, is nothing but a prisoner here himself."

"Oh," said Despereaux. "Um, may I get down, Gregory?"

"The mouse wants to know if Gregory the jailer will let him go. Listen to Gregory, mouse. You do not *want* to be let go. Here, in this dungeon, you are in the treacherous dark heart of the world. And if Gregory were to release you, the twistings and turnings and dead ends and false doorways of this place would swallow you for all eternity.

"Only Gregory and the rats can find their way through this maze. The rats because they know, because the way of it mirrors their own dark hearts. And Gregory because the rope is forever tied to his ankle to guide him back to the beginning. Gregory would let you go, but you would only beg him to take you up again. The rats are coming for you, you see."

"They are?"

"Listen," said Gregory. "You can hear their tails dragging through the muck and filth. You can hear them filing their nails and teeth. They are coming. They are coming to take you apart piece by piece."

Despereaux listened and he was quite certain that he could hear the nails and teeth of the rats, the sound of sharp things being made sharper still.

"They will strip all the fur from your flesh and all the flesh from your bones. When they are done with you, there will be nothing left except red thread. Red thread and bones. Gregory has seen it many times, the tragic end of a mouse."

"But I need to live," said Despereaux. "I cannot die."

"You cannot die. Ah, that is lovely. He says he cannot die!" Gregory closed his hand more tightly around Despereaux. "And why would that be, mouse? Why is it that you cannot die?"

"Because I'm in love. I love somebody and it is my duty to serve her."

"Love," said Gregory. "Love. Hark you, I will show you the twisted results of love." Another match was struck; the candle was lit again, and Gregory held it up so that its flame illuminated a massive, towering, teetering pile of spoons and kettles and soup bowls.

"Look on that, mouse," said Gregory. "That is a monument to the foolishness of love."

"What is it?" asked Despereaux. He stared at the great tower that reached up, up, up into the blackness.

"What it looks like. Spoons. Bowls. Kettles. All of them gathered here as hard evidence of the pain of loving a living thing. The king loved the queen and the queen died; this monstrosity, this junk heap is the result of love."

"I don't understand," said Despereaux.

"And you will not understand until you lose what you love. But enough about love," said Gregory. He blew out the candle. "We will talk instead about your life. And how Gregory will save it, if you so desire."

"Why would you save me?" Despereaux asked. "Have you saved any of the other mice?"

"Go on, mouse," said Gregory. "Tell Gregory a story."

"Never," said Gregory, "not one."

"Why would you save me, then?"

"Because you, mouse, can tell Gregory a story. Stories are light. Light is precious in a world so dark. Begin at the beginning. Tell Gregory a story. Make some light."

And because Despereaux wanted very much to live, he said, "Once upon a time …"

"Yes," said Gregory happily. He raised his hand higher and then higher still until Despereaux's whiskers brushed against his leathery, timeworn ear. "Go on, mouse," said Gregory. "Tell Gregory a story."

And it was in this way that Despereaux became the only mouse sent to the dungeon whom the rats did not reduce to a pile of bones and a piece of red thread.

It was in this way that Despereaux was saved.

Reader, if you don't mind, that is where we will leave our small mouse for now: in the dark of the dungeon, in the hand of an old jailer, telling a story to save himself.

It is time for us to turn our attention elsewhere; time for us, reader, to speak of rats, and of one rat in particular.

Book
THE SECOND

Chiaroscuro

Chapter Sixteen
blinded by the light

AS OUR STORY CONTINUES, reader, we must go backwards in time to the birth of a rat, a rat named Chiaroscuro and called Roscuro, a rat born into the filth and darkness of the dungeon, several years before the mouse Despereaux was born upstairs, in the light.

Reader, do you know the definition of the word "chiaroscuro"? If you look in your dictionary, you will find that it means the arrangement of light and dark, darkness and light together. Rats do not care for light. Roscuro's parents were having a bit of fun when they named their son. Rats have a sense of humour. Rats, in fact, think that life is very funny. And they are right, reader. They are right.

In the case of Chiaroscuro, however, the joke had a hint of prophecy to it, for it happened that when Roscuro was a very young rat, he came upon a great length of rope on the dungeon floor.

"Ah, what have we here?" said Roscuro.

And being a rat, he immediately began to nibble at the rope.

"Stop that," boomed a voice, and a great hand came out of the darkness and picked the rat up by his tail and held him suspended upside down.

"Were you nibbling on Gregory's rope, rat?"

"Who wants to know?" said Roscuro, for even upside down he was still a rat.

"You smart-alecky rat, you smart-alecky rat nib-nib-nibbling on Gregory's rope. Gregory will teach you to mess with his rope."

And keeping Roscuro upside down, Gregory lit a match with the nail of his thumb, *sssssstttttt*, and then held the brilliant flame right in Roscuro's face.

"Aagh," said Roscuro. He pulled his head back, away from the light. But, alas, he did not close his eyes, and the flame exploded around him and danced inside him.

"Has no one told you the rules?" said Gregory.

"What rules?"

"Gregory's rope, rat, is off limits."

"So?"

"Apologize for chewing on Gregory's rope."

"I will not," said Roscuro.

"Apologize."

"No."

"Filthy rat," said Gregory. "You black-souled thing. Gregory has had it with you rats." He held the match closer to Roscuro's face, and a terrible smell of burnt whiskers rose up around the jailer and the rat. And then the match went out and Gregory released Roscuro's tail. He flung him back into the darkness.

"Do not ever touch Gregory's rope again, or you will be sorry."

Roscuro sat on the dungeon floor. The whiskers on the left side of his face were gone. His heart was beating hard, and though the light from the match had disappeared, it danced, still, before the rat's eyes, even when he closed them.

"Light," he said aloud. And then he whispered the word again. "Light."

From that moment on, Roscuro showed an abnormal, inordinate interest in illumination of all sorts. He was always, in the darkness of the dungeon, on the lookout for light – the smallest glimmer, the tiniest shimmer. His rat soul longed inexplicably for it; he began to think that light was the only thing that gave life meaning, and he despaired that there was so little of it to be had.

He finally voiced this sentiment to his friend, a very old one-eared rat named Botticelli Remorso.

"I think," said Roscuro, "that the meaning of life is light."

"Light," said Botticelli. "Ha-ha-ha – you kill me. Light has nothing to do with it."

"What does it all mean, then?" asked Roscuro.

"The meaning of life," said Botticelli, "is suffering, specifically the suffering of others. Prisoners, for instance. Reducing a prisoner to weeping and wailing and begging is a delightful way to invest your existence with meaning."

As he spoke, Botticelli swung, from the one

extraordinarily long nail of his right front paw, a heart-shaped locket. He had taken the locket from a prisoner and hung it on a thin braided rope. Whenever Botticelli spoke, the locket moved. Back and forth, back and forth it swung. "Are you listening?" Botticelli said to Roscuro.

"I am listening."

"Good," said Botticelli. "Do as I say and your life will be full of meaning. This is how to torture a prisoner: first, you must convince him that you are a friend. Listen to him. Encourage him to confess his sins. And when the time is right, talk to him. Tell him what he wants to hear. Tell him, for instance, that you will forgive him. This is a wonderful joke to play upon a prisoner, to promise forgiveness."

"Why?" said Roscuro. His eyes went back and forth, back and forth, following the locket.

"Because," said Botticelli, "you will promise it – ha! – but you will not grant it. You gain his trust. And then you deny him. You refuse to offer the very thing he wants. Forgiveness, freedom, friendship, whatever it is that his heart most desires, you withhold." At this point in his lecture, Botticelli laughed so hard that he had to sit down and catch his breath. The locket swayed slowly back and forth and then stopped altogether.

"Ha," said Botticelli, "ha-ha-ha! You gain his trust, you refuse him and – ha-ha! – you become what he knew you were all along, what *you* knew you were all along, not a friend, not a confessor, not a forgiver, but – ha-ha! – a *rat!*" Botticelli wiped his eyes and shook his head and sighed a sigh of great contentment. He set the locket in motion again. "At that point, it is most effective to run back and forth over the prisoner's feet, inducing physical terror along with the emotional sort. Oh," he said, "it is such a lovely game, such a lovely game! And it is just absolutely chock-full of meaning."

"I would like very much to torture a prisoner," said Roscuro. "I would like to make someone suffer."

"Your time will come," said Botticelli. "Currently, all the prisoners are spoken for. But another prisoner will arrive sooner or later. How do I know this to be true? Because, Roscuro, thankfully there is evil in the world. And the presence of evil guarantees the existence of prisoners."

"So, soon, there will be a prisoner for me?"

"Yes," said Botticelli Remorso. "Yes."

"I'm looking forward to it."

"Ha-ha-ha! Of course you are looking forward to it. You are looking forward to it because you are a rat, a real rat."

"Yes," said Roscuro. "I am a real rat."

"Concerned not at all with the light," said Botticelli.

"Concerned not at all with the light," repeated Roscuro.

Botticelli laughed again and shook his head. The locket, suspended from the long nail on his paw, swung back and forth, back and forth.

"You, my young friend, are a rat. Exactly. Yes. Evil. Prisoners. Rats. Suffering. It all fits together so neatly, so sweetly. Oh, it is a lovely world, a lovely, dark world."

Chapter Seventeen
small comforts

NOT LONG AFTER this conversation between Botticelli and Roscuro, a prisoner did arrive. The dungeon door slammed and the two rats watched a man being led by a king's soldier down the stairs into the dungeon.

"Excellent," whispered Botticelli. "This one is yours."

Roscuro looked at the man closely. "I will make him suffer," he said.

But as he stared up at the man, the door was suddenly flung open and a thick and brilliant shaft of afternoon light cut into the dark of the dungeon.

"Ugh," said Botticelli. He covered his eyes with one paw.

Roscuro, however, stared directly into the light.

Reader, this is important: The rat called Chiaroscuro did not look away. He let the light from the upstairs world enter him and fill him. He gasped aloud with the wonder of it.

"Give him his small comforts," shouted a voice at the top of the stairs, and a red cloth was thrown into the light. The cloth hung suspended for a moment, bright red and glowing, and then the door was slammed shut again and the light disappeared and the cloth fell to the floor. It was Gregory the jailer who bent to pick it up.

"Go on," said the old man as he held out the cloth to the prisoner, "take it. You'll need every last bit of warmth down here."

And so the prisoner took the cloth and draped it around his shoulders as if it were a cloak, and the soldier of the king said, "Right then, Gregory, he's all yours." And the soldier turned and went back up the steps and opened the door to the outside world and some small light leaked in before

Roscuro, however, stared directly into the light.

he closed the door behind him.

"Did you see that?" Roscuro said to Botticelli.

"Hideously ugly," said Botticelli. "Ridiculous. What can they possibly mean by letting all that light in at once. Don't they know that this is a dungeon?"

"It was beautiful," said Roscuro.

"No," said Botticelli. "No." He looked at Roscuro intently. "Not beautiful. No."

"I must see more light. I must see all of it," said Roscuro. "I must go upstairs."

Botticelli sighed. "Who cares about the light? Your obsession with it is tiresome. Listen. We are rats. Rats. We do not like light. We are about darkness. We are about suffering."

"But," said Roscuro, "upstairs…"

"No 'buts,'" said Botticelli. "No 'buts.' None. Rats do not go upstairs. Upstairs is the domain of mice." He took the locket from around his neck.

"What," he said, swinging it back and forth, "is this rope made of?"

"Whiskers."

"The whiskers of whom?"

"Mice."

"Exactly. And who lives upstairs?"

"Mice."

"Exactly. Mice." Botticelli turned his head and spat on the floor. "Mice are nothing but little packages of blood and bones, afraid of everything. They are despicable, laughable, the opposite of everything we strive to be. Do you want to live in their world?"

Roscuro looked up, past Botticelli to the delicious sliver of light that shone out from underneath the door. He said nothing.

"Listen," said Botticelli, "this is what you should do: go and torture the prisoner. Go and take the red cloth from him. The cloth will satisfy your craving for something from that world. But do not go up into the light. You will regret it." As he spoke, the locket swung back and forth, back and forth. "You do not belong in that world. You are a rat. A rat. Say it with me."

"A rat," said Roscuro.

"Ah, but you are cheating. You must say, '*I am* a rat,'" said Botticelli, smiling his slow smile at Roscuro.

"I am a rat," said Roscuro.

"Again," said Botticelli, swinging his locket.

"I am a rat."

"Exactly," said Botticelli. "A rat is a rat is a rat. End of story. World without end. Amen."

"Yes," said Roscuro. "Amen, I am a rat." He closed his eyes. He saw, again, the red cloth spinning against the backdrop of gold.

And he told himself, reader, that it was the cloth that he desired and not the light.

Chapter Eighteen ∽
confessions

ROSCURO WENT, as Botticelli told him he must, to torment the new prisoner and to take the red cloth from him.

The man was sitting with his legs stretched out straight in front of him, chained to the floor. The red cloth was still draped over his shoulders.

Roscuro squeezed through the bars and crept slowly over the damp, weeping stones of the cell floor.

When he was close to the man, he said, "Ah, welcome, welcome. We are delighted to have you."

The man lit a match and looked at Roscuro.

Roscuro stared longingly into the light.

"Go on," said the prisoner. He waved a hand in the direction of Roscuro and the match went out. "Yer nothing but a rat."

"I am," said Roscuro, "exactly that. A rat. Allow me to congratulate you on your very astute powers of observation."

"What do ye want, rat?"

"What do I want? Nothing. Nothing for my sake, that is. I have come for you. I have come to keep you company here in the dark." He crawled closer to the man.

"I don't need the company of a rat."

"What about the solace a sympathetic ear can provide? Do you need that?"

"Huh?"

"Would you like to confess your sins?"

"To a rat? You're kidding, you are."

"Come now," said Roscuro. "Close your eyes. Pretend that I am not a rat. Pretend that I am nothing but a voice in the darkness. A voice that cares."

The prisoner closed his eyes. "All right," he said. "I'll tell you. But I'm telling you because there ain't no point in *not* telling you, no point in keeping secrets from a dirty little rat. I ain't in such a desperate way that I need to lie to a rat."

The man cleared his throat. "I'm here for stealing six cows, two Jerseys and four Guernseys. Cow theft, that's my crime." He opened his eyes and stared into the darkness. He laughed. He closed his eyes again. "But there's something else I done, many years ago, another crime, and they don't even know of it."

"Go on," said Roscuro softly. He crept closer. He allowed one paw to touch the magical red cloth.

"I traded my girl, my own daughter, for this red tablecloth and for a hen and for a handful of cigarettes."

"Tsk," said Roscuro. He was not alarmed to hear of such a hideous thing. His parents, after all, had not much cared for him, and certainly, if there had been any profit in it, they would have sold him. And then, too, Botticelli Remorso, one lazy Sunday afternoon, had recited from memory all the confessions he had heard from prisoners. What humans were capable of came as no surprise to Roscuro.

"And then…" said the man.

"And then," encouraged Roscuro.

"And then I done the worst thing of all: I walked away from her and she was crying and calling out for me and I did not even look back. I did not. Oh, Lord, I kept walking." The prisoner cleared his throat. He sniffed.

"Ah," said Roscuro. "Yes. I see." By now he was standing so that all four of his paws were touching the red cloth.

"Do you find comfort in this cloth that you sold your child for?"

"It's warm," said the man.

"Was it worth your child?"

"I like the colour of it."

"Does the cloth remind you of what you have done wrong?"

"It does," the prisoner said. He sniffed. "It does."

"Allow me to ease your burden," said Roscuro. He stood on his hind legs and bowed at the waist. "I will take this reminder of your sin from you," he said. The rat took hold of the tablecloth in his strong teeth and pulled it off the shoulders of the man.

"Hey, see here. I want that back."

But Roscuro, reader, was quick. He pulled the tablecloth through the bars of the cell, *whoosh*, like a magic trick in reverse.

"Hey!" shouted the prisoner. "Bring that back. It's all I got."

"Yes," said Roscuro, "and that is exactly why I must have it."

"You dirty rat!" shouted the prisoner.

"Yes," said Roscuro. "That is right. That is most accurate."

And he left the man and dragged the tablecloth back to his nest and considered it.

What a disappointment it was! Looking at it, Roscuro knew that Botticelli was wrong. What Roscuro wanted, what he needed, was not the cloth, but the light that had shone behind it.

He wanted to be filled, flooded, blinded again with light.

And for that, reader, the rat knew that he must go upstairs.

Chapter Nineteen
light, light everywhere

IMAGINE, IF YOU WILL, having spent the whole of your life in a dungeon. Imagine that late one spring day you step out of the dark and into a world of bright windows and polished floors, winking copper pots, shining suits of armour and tapestries sewn in gold.

Imagine. And while you are imagining things, imagine this, too. Imagine that at the same time as the rat steps from the dungeon and into the castle, a mouse is being born upstairs – a mouse, reader, who is destined to meet the light-bedazzled rat.

But that meeting will occur much later, and for

now, the rat is nothing but happy, delighted, amazed to find himself standing in so much light.

"I," said Roscuro, spinning dizzily from one bright thing to the next, "will never leave. No, never. I will never go back to the dungeon. Why would I? I will never torture another prisoner. It is here that I belong."

The rat waltzed happily from room to room until he found himself at the door to the banquet hall. He looked inside and saw gathered there King Phillip, Queen Rosemary, the Princess Pea, twenty noble people, a juggler, four minstrels and all the king's men. This party, reader, was a sight for a rat's eyes. Roscuro had never seen happy people. He had known only the miserable ones. Gregory the jailer and those who were consigned to his domain did not laugh or smile or clink glasses with the person sitting next to them.

Roscuro was enchanted. Everything glittered. Everything. The gold spoons on the table and the jingle bells on the juggler's cap, the strings on the minstrels' guitars and the crowns on the king's and the queen's heads.

And the little princess! How lovely she was! How much like light itself. Her gown was covered in sequins that winked and glimmered at the rat. And when she laughed, and she laughed often, everything around her seemed to glow brighter.

"Oh, really," said Roscuro, "this is too extraordinary. This is too wonderful. I must tell Botticelli that he was wrong. Suffering is not the answer. *Light* is the answer."

And he made his way into the banquet hall. He lifted his tail off the ground and held it at an angle and marched in time to the music the minstrels were playing on their guitars.

The rat, reader, invited himself to the party.

Chapter Twenty
a view from a chandelier

THERE WAS, in the banquet hall, a most beautiful and ornate chandelier. The crystals that hung from it caught the light of the candles on the table and the light from the face of the laughing princess. They danced to the rhythm of the minstrels' music, swaying back and forth, twinkling and beckoning. What better place to view all this glory, all this beauty?

There was so much laughing and singing and juggling that no one noticed as Roscuro crawled up a table leg and onto the table, and from there flung himself onto the lowest branch of the chandelier.

Hanging by one paw he swung back and forth, admiring the spectacle below him: the smells of the food, the sound of the music, and the light, the light, the light. Amazing. Unbelievable. Roscuro smiled and shook his head.

Unfortunately, a rat can hang from a chandelier for only so long before he is discovered. This would be true at even the loudest party.

Reader, do you know who it was that spotted him?

You're right.

The sharp-eyed Princess Pea.

"A rat!" she shouted. "A rat is hanging from the chandelier!"

The party, as I have noted, was loud. The minstrels were strumming and singing. The people were laughing and eating. The man with the jingle cap was juggling and jingling.

No one, in the midst of all this merriment, heard the Pea. No one except for Roscuro.

Rat.

He had never before been aware of what an ugly word it was.

"A rat!" she shouted.
"A rat is hanging from the chandelier!"

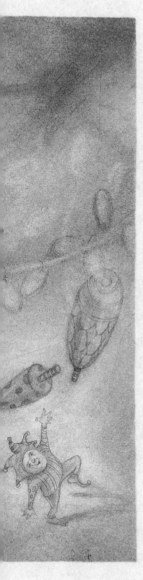

Rat.

In the middle of all that beauty it immediately became clear that it was an extremely distasteful syllable.

Rat.

A curse, an insult, a word totally without light. And not until he heard it from the mouth of the princess did Roscuro realize that he did not like being a rat, that he did not want to be a rat. This revelation hit Roscuro with such force that it made him lose his grip on the chandelier.

The rat, reader, fell.

And, alas, he fell, directly into the queen's bowl of soup.

Chapter Twenty-one ∾
the queen's last words

THE QUEEN LOVED SOUP. She loved
soup more than anything in the world except for the
Princess Pea and the king. And because the queen
loved it, soup was served in the castle for every banquet, every lunch and every dinner.

And what soup it was! Cook's love and admira-
tion for the queen and her palate moved the broth
that she concocted from the level of mere food to a
high art.

On this particular day, for this particular banquet,
Cook had outdone herself. The soup was a master-
work, a delicate mingling of chicken, watercress

and garlic. Roscuro, as he surfaced from the bottom of the queen's capacious bowl, could not help taking a few appreciative sips.

"Lovely," he said, distracted for a moment from the misery of his existence. "Delightful."

"See?" shouted the Pea. "See!" She stood. She pointed her finger right at Roscuro. "It is a rat. I told you that it was a rat. He was hanging from the chandelier, and now he is in Mama's soup!"

The musicians stopped playing their guitars. The juggler stopped juggling. The noble people stopped eating.

The queen looked at Roscuro.

Roscuro looked at the queen.

Reader, in the spirit of honesty I must utter a difficult and unsavoury truth: Rats are not beautiful creatures. They are not even cute. They are, really, rather nasty beasts, particularly if one happens to appear in your bowl of soup with pieces of watercress clinging to his whiskers.

There was a long moment of silence, and then Roscuro said to the queen, "I beg your pardon."

In response, the queen flung her spoon in the

air and made an incredible noise, a noise that was in no way worthy of a queen, a noise somewhere between the neigh of a horse and the squeal of a pig, a noise that sounded something like this: *neiggghh-hhiiiinnnnkkkkkk.*

And then she said, "There is a rat in my soup."

The queen was really a simple soul and always, her whole life, had done nothing except state the overly obvious.

She died as she lived.

"There is a rat in my soup" were the last words she uttered. She clutched her chest and fell over backwards. Her royal chair hit the floor with a thump, and the banquet hall exploded. Spoons were dropped. Chairs were flung back.

"Save her!" thundered the king. "You must save her!"

All the king's men ran to try and rescue the queen.

Roscuro climbed out of the bowl of soup. He felt that, under the circumstances, it would be best if he left. As he crawled across the tablecloth he remembered the words of the prisoner in the dungeon, his regret that he did not look back at his daughter as he left her. And so, Roscuro turned.

He looked back.

And he saw that the princess was glaring at him. Her eyes were filled with disgust and anger.

"Go back to the dungeon" was what the look she gave him said. "Go back into the darkness where you belong."

This look, reader, broke Roscuro's heart.

Did you think that rats do not have hearts? Wrong. All living things have a heart. And the heart of any living thing can be broken.

If the rat had not looked over his shoulder, perhaps his heart would not have broken. And it is possible, then, that I would not have a story to tell.

But, reader, he did look.

Chapter Twenty-two
he puts his heart together again

ROSCURO HURRIED from the banquet hall.

"A rat," he said. He put a paw over his heart. "I am a rat. And there is no light for rats. There will be no light for me."

The king's men were still bent over the queen. The king was still shouting, "Save her! Save her!" And the queen was still dead, of course, when Roscuro encountered the queen's royal soup spoon lying on the floor.

"I will have something beautiful," he said aloud. "I am a rat, but I will have something beautiful.

*"I will have something beautiful.
And I will have revenge."*

I will have a crown of my own." He picked up the spoon. He put it on his head.

"Yes," said Roscuro. "I will have something beautiful. And I will have revenge. Both things. Somehow."

There are those hearts, reader, that never mend again once they are broken. Or if they do mend, they heal themselves in a crooked and lopsided way, as if sewn together by a careless craftsman. Such was the fate of Chiaroscuro. His heart was broken. Picking up the spoon and placing it on his head, speaking of revenge, these things helped him to put his heart together again. But it was, alas, put together wrong.

"Where is the rat?" shouted the king. "Find that rat!"

"If you want me," muttered Roscuro as he left the banquet hall, "I will be in the dungeon, in the darkness."

Chapter Twenty-three
consequences

THERE WERE, OF COURSE, dire consequences of Roscuro's behaviour. Every action, reader, no matter how small, has a consequence. For instance, the young Roscuro gnawed on Gregory the jailer's rope, and because he gnawed on the rope, a match was lit in his face, and because a match was lit in his face, his soul was set afire.

The rat's soul was set afire, and because of this he journeyed upstairs, seeking the light. Upstairs, in the banquet hall, the Princess Pea spotted him and called out the word "rat", and because of this Roscuro fell into the queen's soup. And because the rat fell into the queen's soup, the queen died. You can see, can't you, how everything is related to everything else? You can see, quite clearly, how every action has a consequence.

For instance (if, reader, you will indulge me, and allow me to continue this meditation on consequences), because the queen died while eating soup, the heartbroken king outlawed soup; and because soup was outlawed, so were all the instruments involved in the making and eating of soup: spoons and bowls and kettles. These things were collected from all the people of the Kingdom of Dor, and they were piled in the dungeon.

And because Roscuro was dazzled by the light of one match and journeyed upstairs and fell into the queen's soup and the queen died, the king ordered the death of every rat in the land.

The king's men went bravely into the dungeon to kill the rats. But the thing about killing a rat is that you must first *find* a rat. And if a rat does not want to be found, reader, he will not be found.

The king's men succeeded only in getting lost in the dungeon's tortuous mazes. Some of them, in fact, did not ever find their way out again and died there in the dark heart of the castle. And so, the killing of all rats was not successful. And in desperation, King Phillip declared that rats were illegal. He declared them outlaws.

This, of course, was a ridiculous law, as rats are outlaws to begin with. How can you outlaw an outlaw? It is a waste of time and energy. But still, the king officially decreed that all rats in the Kingdom of Dor were outlaws and should be treated as such. When you are a king, you may make as many ridiculous laws as you like. That is what being a king is all about.

But, reader, we must not forget that King Phillip loved the queen and that without her he was lost. This is the danger of loving: No matter how powerful you are, no matter how many kingdoms you rule, you cannot stop those you love from dying. Making soup illegal, outlawing rats, these things soothed the poor king's heart. And so we must forgive him.

And what of the outlawed rats? What of one outlawed rat in particular?

What of Chiaroscuro?

In the darkness of the dungeon, he sat in his nest with the spoon atop his head. He set to work fashioning for himself a kingly cape made out of a scrap of the red tablecloth. And as he worked, old one-eared Botticelli Remorso sat next to him swinging his locket back and forth, back and forth, saying, "You see what comes from a rat going upstairs? I hope that you have learnt your lesson. Your job in this world is to make others suffer."

"Yes," muttered Roscuro. "Yes. That is exactly what I intend to do. I will make the princess suffer for how she looked at me."

And as Roscuro worked and planned, the jailer Gregory held tight to his rope and made his own way through the darkness, and in a dank cell, the prisoner who had once had a red tablecloth and now had nothing spent his days and nights weeping quietly.

High above the dungeon, upstairs, in the castle, a small mouse stood alone one evening as his brothers and sisters sniffed for crumbs. He stood with his head cocked to one side, listening to a sweet sound he did not yet have a name for. There would be consequences of the mouse's love for music. You, reader, know already some of those consequences. Because of the music, the mouse would find his way to a princess. He would fall in love.

And speaking of consequences, the same evening that Despereaux stood inside the castle hearing music for the first time, outside the castle, in the gloom of dusk, more consequences drew near. A wagon driven by a king's soldier and piled high with spoons and bowls and kettles, was making its way to the castle. And beside the soldier there sat a young girl with ears that looked like nothing so much as pieces of cauliflower stuck on either side of her head.

The girl's name, reader, was Miggery Sow. And though she did not yet know it, she would be instrumental in helping the rat work his revenge.

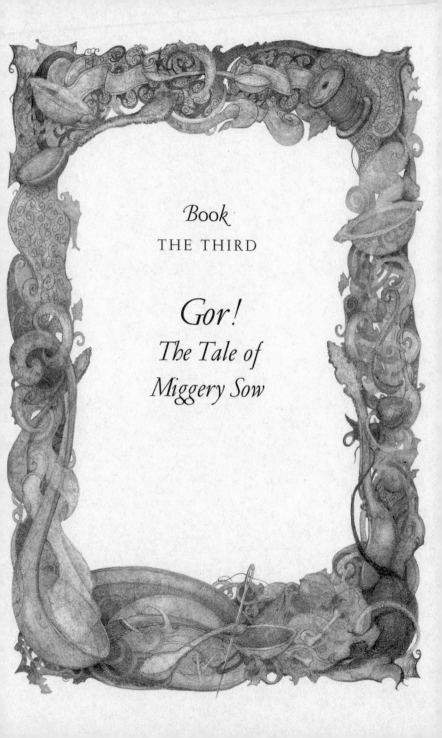

Book
THE THIRD

Gor!
The Tale of
Miggery Sow

Chapter Twenty-four
a handful of cigarettes,
a red tablecloth and a hen

AGAIN, READER, we must go backwards before we can go forwards. With that said, here begins a short history of the life and times of Miggery Sow, a girl born into this world many years before the mouse Despereaux and the rat Chiaroscuro, a girl born far from the castle, a girl named for her father's favourite prize-winning pig.

Miggery Sow was six years old when her mother, holding onto Mig's hand and staring directly into Mig's eyes, died.

"Ma?" said Mig. "Ma, couldn't you stay here with me?"

"Oh," said her mother. "Who is that? Who is that holding my hand?"

"It's me, Ma, Miggery Sow."

"Ah, child, let me go."

"But I want you to stay here," said Mig, wiping first at her runny nose and then at her runny eyes.

"You want," said her mother.

"Yes," said Mig, "I want."

"Ah, child, and what does it matter what you are wanting?" said her mother. She squeezed Mig's hand once, twice, and then she died, leaving Mig alone with her father, who, on a market day in spring soon after his wife's death, sold his daughter into service for a handful of cigarettes, a red table-cloth and a hen.

"Papa?" said Mig, when her father was walking away from her with the hen in his arms, a cigarette in his mouth and the red tablecloth draped across his shoulders like a cape.

"Go on, Mig," he said. "You belong to that man now."

"But I don't want to, Papa," she said. "I want to go with you." She took hold of the red tablecloth and tugged on it.

"Lord, child," her father said, "and who is asking you what you want? Go on now." He untangled her fingers from the cloth and turned her in the direction of the man who had bought her.

Mig watched her father walk away, the red tablecloth billowing out behind him. He left his daughter. And, reader, as you already know, he did not look back. Not even once.

Can you imagine it? Can you imagine your father selling you for a tablecloth, a hen and a handful of cigarettes? Close your eyes, please, and consider it for just a moment.

Done?

I hope that the hair on the back of your neck stood up as you thought of Mig's fate and how it would be if it were your own.

Poor Mig. What will become of her? You must, frightened though you may be, read on and see for yourself.

Reader, it is your duty.

Chapter Twenty-five
a vicious circle

MIGGERY SOW called the man who purchased her Uncle, as he said she must. And also, as he said she must, Mig tended Uncle's sheep and cooked Uncle's food and scrubbed Uncle's kettle. She did all of this without a word of thanks or praise from the man himself.

Another unfortunate fact of life with Uncle was that he very much liked giving Mig what he referred to as "a good clout to the ear". In fairness to Uncle, it must be reported that he did always enquire whether or not Mig was interested in receiving the clout.

Their daily exchanges went something like this:

Uncle: "I thought I told you to clean the kettle."

Mig: "I cleaned it, Uncle. I cleaned it good."

Uncle: "Ah, it's filthy. You'll have to be punished, won't ye?"

Mig: "Gor, Uncle, I cleaned the kettle."

Uncle: "Are ye saying that I'm a liar, girl?"

Mig: "No, Uncle."

Uncle: "Do ye want a good clout to the ear, then?"

Mig: "No, thank you, Uncle, I don't."

Alas, Uncle seemed to be as entirely unconcerned with what Mig wanted as her mother and father had been. The discussed clout to the ear was always delivered ... delivered, I am afraid, with a great deal of enthusiasm on Uncle's part, and received with absolutely no enthusiasm at all on the part of Mig.

These clouts were alarmingly frequent. And Uncle was scrupulously fair in paying attention to both the right and left side of Miggery Sow. So it was that after a time the young Mig's ears came to resemble not so much ears as pieces of cauliflower stuck to either side of her head.

And they became about as useful to her as pieces

of cauliflower. That is to say that they all but ceased their functioning as ears. Words, for Mig, lost their sharp edges. And then they lost their edges altogether and became blurry, blankety things that she had a great deal of trouble making any sense out of at all.

The less Mig heard, the less she understood. The less she understood, the more things she did wrong; and the more things she did wrong, the more clouts to the ear she received, and the less she heard. This is what is known as a vicious circle. And Miggery Sow was right in the centre of it.

Which is not, reader, where anybody would want to be.

But then, as you know, what Miggery Sow wanted had never been of much concern to anyone.

Chapter Twenty-six
royalty

WHEN MIG TURNED SEVEN years old there was no cake, no celebration, no singing, no present, no acknowledgement of her birthday at all other than Mig saying, "Uncle, today I am seven years old."

And Uncle saying in return, "Did I ask ye how old you were today? Get out of my face before I give ye a good clout to the ear."

A few hours after receiving her birthday clout to the ear, Mig was out in the field with Uncle's sheep when she saw something glittering and glowing on the horizon.

She thought for a moment that it was the sun. But she turned and saw that the sun was in the west, where it should be, sinking to join the earth. This thing that shone so brightly was something else. Mig stood in the field and shaded her eyes with her left hand and watched the brilliant light draw closer and closer and closer until it revealed itself to be King Phillip and his Queen Rosemary and their daughter, the young Princess Pea.

The royal family was surrounded by knights in shining armour and horses in shining armour. And atop each member of the royal family's head there was a golden crown, and they were all, the king and the queen and the princess, dressed in robes decorated with jewels and sequins that glittered and glowed and captured the light of the setting sun and reflected it back.

"Gor," breathed Mig.

The Princess Pea was riding on a white horse that picked up its legs very high and set them down very daintily. The Pea saw Mig standing and staring, and she raised a hand to her.

"Hello," the Princess Pea called out merrily,

"Gor," breathed Mig.

"hello." And she waved her hand again.

Mig did not wave back; instead, she stood and watched, open-mouthed, as the perfect, beautiful family passed her by.

"Papa," called the princess to the king, "what is wrong with the girl? She will not wave to me."

"Never mind," said the king. "It is of no consequence, my dear."

"But I am a princess. And I waved to her. She should wave back."

Mig, for her part, continued to stare. Looking at the royal family had awakened some deep and slumbering need in her; it was as if a small candle had been lit in her interior, sparked to life by the brilliance of the king and the queen and the princess.

For the first time in her life, reader, Mig hoped.

And hope is like love … a ridiculous, wonderful, powerful thing.

Mig tried to name this strange emotion; she put a hand up to touch one of her aching ears, and she realized that the feeling she was experiencing, the hope blooming inside of her, felt exactly the opposite of a good clout.

She smiled and took her hand away from her ear. She waved to the princess. "Today is my birthday!" Mig called out.

But the king and the queen and the princess were by now too far away to hear her.

"Today," shouted Mig, "I am seven years old!"

Chapter Twenty-seven
a wish

THAT NIGHT, in the small, dark hut that she shared with Uncle and the sheep, Mig tried to speak of what she had seen.

"Uncle?" she said.

"Eh?"

"I saw some human stars today."

"How's that?"

"I saw them all glittering and glowing, and there was a little princess wearing her own crown and riding on a little white, tippy-toed horse."

"What are ye going on about?" said Uncle.

"I saw a king and a queen and a itty-bitty princess," shouted Mig.

"So?" shouted Uncle back.

"I would like…" said Mig shyly. "I wish to be one of them princesses."

"Har," laughed Uncle. "Har. An ugly, dumb thing like you? You ain't even worth the enormous lot I paid for you. Don't I wish every night that I had back that good hen and that red tablecloth in place of you?"

He did not wait for Mig to guess the answer to this question. "I do," he said. "I wish it every night. That tablecloth was the colour of blood. That hen could lay eggs like nobody's business."

"I want to be a princess," said Mig. "I want to wear a crown."

"A crown." Uncle laughed. "She wants to wear a crown." He laughed harder. He took the empty kettle and put it atop his head. "Look at me," he said. "I'm a king. See my crown? I'm a king just like I've always wanted to be. I'm a king because I *want* to be one."

He danced around the hut with the kettle on

his head. He laughed until he cried. And then he stopped dancing and took the kettle from his head and looked at Mig and said, "Do ye want a good clout to the ear for such nonsense?"

"No, thank you, Uncle," said Mig.

But she got one anyway.

"Look here," said Uncle after the clout had been delivered. "We will hear no more talk of princesses. Besides, who ever asked you what you wanted in this world, girl?"

The answer to that question, reader, as you well know, was absolutely no one.

Chapter Twenty-eight
to the castle

YEARS PASSED. Mig spent them scrubbing the kettle and tending the sheep and cleaning the hut and collecting innumerable, uncountable, extremely painful clouts to the ear. In the evening, spring or winter, summer or fall, Mig stood in the field as the sun set, hoping that the royal family would pass before her again.

"Gor, I would like to see that little princess another time, wouldn't I? And her little pony, too, with his tippy-toed feet." This hope, this wish, that she would see the princess again, was lodged deep in Mig's heart; lodged firmly right next to it was the hope that she, Miggery Sow, could someday become a princess herself.

The first of Mig's wishes was granted, in a round-about way, when King Phillip outlawed soup. The king's men were sent out to deliver the grim news and to collect from the people of the Kingdom of Dor their kettles, their spoons and their bowls.

Reader, you know exactly how and why this law came to pass, so you would not be as surprised as Uncle was when, one Sunday, a soldier of the king knocked on the door of the hut that Mig and Uncle and the sheep shared and announced that soup was against the law.

"How's that?" said Uncle.

"By royal order of King Phillip," repeated the soldier, "I am sent here to tell you that soup has been outlawed in the Kingdom of Dor. You will, by order of the king, never again consume soup. Nor will you think of it or talk about it. And I, as one of the king's loyal servants, am here to take from you your spoons, your kettle and your bowls."

"But that can't be," said Uncle.

"Nevertheless, it is."

"What'll we eat? And what'll we eat it with?"

"Cake," suggested the soldier, "with a fork."

"And wouldn't that be lovely," said Uncle, "if we could afford to eat cake."

The soldier shrugged. "I am only doing my duty. Please hand over your spoons, your bowls and your kettle."

Uncle grabbed hold of his beard. He let go of his beard and grabbed the hair on his head. "Unbelievable!" he shouted. "I suppose next the king will be wanting my sheep and my girl, seeing as those are the only possessions I have left."

"Do you own a girl?" said the soldier.

"I do," said Uncle. "A worthless one, but still, she is mine."

"Ah," said the soldier, "that, I am afraid, is against the law too; no human may own another in the Kingdom of Dor."

"But I paid for her fair and square with a good laying hen and a handful of cigarettes and a blood-red tablecloth."

"No matter," said the soldier. "It is against the law to own another. Now, you will hand over to me, if you please, your spoons, your bowls, your kettle *and* your girl. Or if you choose not to hand over these things then you will come with me to be imprisoned in the castle dungeon. Which will it be?"

And that is how Miggery Sow came to be sitting in a wagon full of soup-related items, next to a soldier of the king.

"Do you have parents?" said the soldier. "I will return you to them."

"Eh?"

"A ma?" shouted the soldier.

"Dead!" said Mig.

"Your pa?" shouted the soldier.

"I ain't seen him since he sold me."

"Right. I'll take you to the castle then."

"Gor," said Mig, looking around the wagon in confusion. "You want me to paddle?"

"To the castle!" shouted the soldier. "I'll take you to the castle."

"The castle? Where the itty-bitty princess lives?"

"That's right."

"Gor," said Mig, "I aim to be a princess, too, someday."

"That's a fine dream," said the solider. He clucked to the horse and tapped the reins and they took off.

"I'm happy to be going," said Mig, putting a hand up and gently touching one of her cauliflower ears.

"Might just as well be happy, seeing as it doesn't make a difference to anyone but you if you are or not," said the soldier. "We will take you to the castle and they will set you up fine. You will no longer be a slave. You will be a paid servant."

"Eh?" said Mig.

"You will be a servant!" shouted the soldier. "Not a slave!"

"Gor!" said Mig, satisfied. "A servant I will be, not a slave."

She was twelve years old. Her mother was dead. Her father had sold her. Her Uncle, who wasn't her uncle at all, had clouted her until she was almost deaf. And she wanted, more than anything in the world, to be a little princess wearing a golden crown and riding a high-stepping white horse.

Reader, do you think that it is a terrible thing to hope when there is really no reason to hope at all? Or is it (as the soldier said about happiness) something that you might just as well do, since, in the end, it really makes no difference to anyone but you?

Chapter Twenty-nine
start with the cursy and finish with the thread

MIGGERY SOW'S LUCK CONTIN-
UED. On her first day on the job as a castle servant
she was sent to deliver a spool of red thread to the
princess.

"Mind," said the head of the serving staff, a dour
woman named Louise, "she is royalty, so you must
make sure you curtsy."

"How's that?" shouted Mig.

"You must curtsy!" shouted Louise.

"Gor," said Mig, "yes'm."

She took the spool of thread from Louise and

made her way up the golden stairs to the princess's room, talking to herself as she went.

"Here I am, off to see the princess. Me, Miggery Sow, seeing the princess up close and personal like. And first off, I must cursy because she is the royalty."

At the door to the princess's room, Mig had a sudden crisis of confidence. She stood a moment, clutching the spool of thread and muttering to herself.

"Now, how did that go?" she said. "Give the princess the thread and then give her a cursy? No, no, first the cursy and then the thread. That's it. Gor, that's right, that's the order. Start with the cursy and finish with the thread."

She knocked at the princess's door.

"Enter," said the Pea.

Mig, hearing nothing, knocked again.

"Enter," said the Pea.

And Mig, still hearing nothing, knocked yet again. "Maybe," she said to herself, "the princess ain't home."

But then the door was flung wide and there was the princess herself, staring right at Miggery Sow.

"Gor," said Mig, her mouth hanging open.

"Hello," said the Pea. "Are you the new serving maid? Have you brought me my thread?"

"Cursy I must!" shouted Mig.

She gathered her skirts, dropped the spool of thread, stuck a foot out and stepped on the spool, rocked back and forth for what seemed like quite a long time (both to the watching princess and the rocking Mig), and finally fell to the floor with a Miggish thud.

"Whoopsie," said Miggery Sow.

The Pea could not help it – she laughed. "That's all right," she said to Mig, shaking her head. "It's the spirit of the thing that counts."

"How's that?" shouted Mig.

"It's the spirit of the thing that counts!" shouted Pea.

"Thank you, miss," said Mig. She got slowly to her feet. She looked at the princess. She looked down at the floor. "First the cursy and then the thread," Mig muttered.

"Pardon?" said the Pea.

"Gor!" said Mig. "The thread!" She dropped to

"Whoopsie," said Miggery Sow.

her hands and knees to locate the spool of thread; when she found it, she stood back up and offered it to Pea. "I brought you yer thread, didn't I?"

"Lovely," said the princess as she took the thread from Mig. "Thank you so much. I cannot seem to hold onto a spool of red thread. Every one I have disappears somehow."

"Are you making a thing?" asked Mig, squinting at the cloth in the Pea's hand.

"I am making a history of the world, my world," said the Pea, "in tapestry. See? Here is my father, the king. And he is playing the guitar because that is something he loves to do and does quite well. And here is my mother, the queen, and she is eating soup because she loved soup."

"Soup! Gor! That's against the law."

"Yes," said the princess, "my father outlawed it because my mother died while she was eating it."

"Your ma's dead?"

"Yes," said the Pea. "She died just last month." She bit her bottom lip to stop it from trembling.

"Ain't that the thing?" said Mig. "My ma is dead too."

"How old were you when she died?"

"Bold was I?" said Mig, taking a step back, away from the princess. "I'm sorry, then."

"No, no, how *old*. How *old* were you?" shouted the Pea.

"Not but six," said Mig.

"I'm sorry," said the princess. She gave Mig a quick, deep look of sympathy. "How old are you now?"

"Twelve years."

"So am I," said the princess. "We're the same age. What is your name?" she shouted.

"Miggery. Miggery Sow, but most just calls me Mig. And I saw you once before, Princess. You passed me by on a little white horse. On my birthday, it was, and I was in the field with Uncle's sheep and it was sunset time."

"Did I wave to you?" asked the princess.

"Eh?"

"Did I wave?" shouted the Pea.

"Yes," nodded Mig.

"But you didn't wave back," said the princess.

"I did," said Mig. "Only you didn't see. Someday,

I will sit on a little white horse and wear a crown and wave. Someday," said Mig, and she put up a hand to touch her left ear, "I will be a princess too."

"Really?" said the Pea. And she gave Mig another quick, deep look, but said nothing else.

When Mig finally made her way back down the golden stairs, Louise was waiting for her.

"How long," she roared, "did it take you to deliver a spool of thread to the princess?"

"Too long?" guessed Mig.

"That's right," said Louise. And she gave Mig a good clout to the ear. "You are not destined to be one of our star servants. That is already abundantly clear."

"No, ma'am," said Mig. "That's all right, though, because I aim to be a princess."

"You? A princess? Don't make me laugh."

This, reader, was a little joke on Louise's part, as she was not a person who laughed. Ever. Not even at a notion as ridiculous as Miggery Sow becoming a princess.

Chapter Thirty
to the dungeon

AT THE CASTLE, for the first time in her young life, Mig had enough to eat. And eat she did. She quickly became plump and then plumper still. She grew rounder and rounder and bigger and bigger. Only her head stayed small.

Reader, as the teller of this tale it is my duty from time to time to utter some hard and rather disagreeable truths. In the spirit of honesty, then, I must inform you that Mig was the tiniest bit lazy. And, too, she was not the sharpest knife in the drawer. That is, she was a bit slow-witted.

Because of these shortcomings, Louise was

hard-pressed to find a job that Miggery Sow could effectively perform. In quick succession, Mig failed as a lady-in-waiting (she was caught trying on the gown of a visiting duchess), a seamstress (she sewed the cloak of the riding master to her own frock and ruined both), and a chambermaid (sent to clean a room, she stood, open-mouthed and delighted, admiring the gold walls and floors and tapestries, exclaiming over and over again, "Gor, ain't it pretty? Gor, ain't it something, then?" and did no cleaning at all).

And while Mig was trying and failing at these many domestic chores, other important things were happening in the castle: The rat, in the dungeon below, was pacing and muttering in the darkness, waiting to take his revenge on the princess. And upstairs in the castle, the princess had met a mouse. And the mouse had fallen in love with her.

Will there be consequences? You bet.

Just as Mig's inability to perform any job well had its consequences. For, finally, as a last resort, Louise sent Mig to the kitchen, where Cook had a reputation for dealing effectively with difficult help.

In Cook's kitchen Mig dropped eggshells in the pound-cake batter; she scrubbed the kitchen floor with cooking oil instead of cleaner; she sneezed directly on the king's pork chop, moments before it was to be served to him.

"Of all the good-for-nothings I have encountered," shouted Cook, "surely you are the worst, the most cauliflower-eared, the good-for-nothing-est. There's only one place left for you. The dungeon."

"Eh?" said Mig, cupping a hand around her ear.

"You are being sent to the dungeon. You are to take the jailer his noonday meal. That will be your duty from now on."

Reader, you know that the mice of the castle feared the dungeon. Must I tell you that the humans feared it too? Certainly it was never far from their thoughts. In the warm months, a foul odour rose out of its dark depths and permeated the whole of the castle. And in the still, cold nights of winter, terrible howls issued from the dark place, as if the castle itself were weeping and moaning.

"It's only the wind," the people of the castle assured each other, "nothing but the wind."

"There's only one place left for you. The dungeon."

Many a serving girl had been sent to the dungeon bearing the jailer's meal only to return white-faced and weeping, hands trembling, teeth chattering, insisting that they would never go back. And worse, there were whispered stories of those servant girls who had been given the job of feeding the jailer, who had gone down the stairs and into the dungeon and who had never been seen or heard from again.

Do you believe that this will be Mig's fate?

Gor! I hope not. What kind of a story would this be without Mig?

"Listen, you cauliflower-eared fool!" shouted Cook. "This is what you do. You take the tray of food down to the dungeon and you wait for the old man to eat the food and then you bring the tray back up. Do you think that you can manage that?"

"Aye, I reckon so," said Mig. "I take the old man the tray and he eats what's on it and then I bring the tray back up. Empty it would be then. I bring the empty tray back up from the deep downs."

"That's right," said Cook. "Seems simple, don't it? But I'm sure you'll find a way to bungle it."

"Eh?" said Mig.

"Nothing," said Cook. "Good luck to you. You'll be needing it."

She watched as Mig descended the dungeon stairs. They were the very same stairs, reader, that the mouse Despereaux had been pushed down the day before. Unlike the mouse, however, Mig had a light: on the tray with the food there was a single, flickering candle to show her the way. She turned on the stairs and looked back at Cook and smiled.

"That cauliflower-eared, good-for-nothing fool," said Cook, shaking her head. "What's to become of someone who goes into the dungeon smiling, I ask you?"

Reader, for the answer to Cook's question you must read on.

Chapter Thirty-one
a song in the dark

THE TERRIBLE FOUL ODOUR of the dungeon did not bother Mig. Perhaps that is because, sometimes, when Uncle had been giving her a good clout to the ear, he had missed his mark and delivered a good clout to Mig's nose instead. This had happened often enough that it interrupted the proper workings of Mig's olfactory senses. And so it was that the overwhelming stench of despair and hopelessness and evil was not at all discernible to her, and she went happily down the twisting and turning stairs.

"Gor!" she shouted. "It's dark, ain't it?"

"Yes, it is Mig," she answered herself, "but if I was a princess, I would be so glittery light-like, there wouldn't be a place in the world that was dark to me."

At this point, Miggery Sow broke into a little song that went something like this:

"I ain't the Princess Pea
But someday I will be,
The Pea, ha-hee.
Someday, I will be."

Mig, as you can imagine, wasn't much of a singer, more of a bellower, really. But in her little song there was, to the rightly tuned ear, a certain kind of music. And as Mig went singing down the stairs of the dungeon there appeared from the shadows a rat wrapped in a cloak of red and wearing a spoon on his head.

"Yes, yes," whispered the rat, "a lovely song. Just the song I have been waiting to hear."

And Roscuro quietly fell in step beside Miggery Sow.

At the bottom of the stairs, Mig shouted out into the darkness, "Gor, it's me, Miggery Sow, most calls me Mig, delivering your food! Come and get it, Mr Deep Downs!"

There was no response.

The dungeon was quiet, but it was not quiet in a good way. It was quiet in an ominous way; it was quiet in the way of small, frightening sounds. There was the snail-like slither of water oozing down the walls and from around a darkened corner there came the low moan of someone in pain. And then, too, there was the noise of the rats going about their business, their sharp nails hitting the stones of the dungeon and their long tails dragging behind them, through the blood and muck.

Reader, if you were standing in the dungeon you would certainly hear all of these disturbing and ominous sounds.

If I were standing in the dungeon, *I* would hear these sounds.

If we were standing together in the dungeon, we would hear these sounds and we would be very frightened; we would cling to each other in our fear.

But what did Miggery Sow hear?

That's right.

Absolutely nothing.

And so she was not afraid at all, not in the least.

She held the tray up higher, and the candle shed its weak light on the towering pile of spoons and bowls and kettles. "Gor," said Mig, "look at them things. I ain't never imagined there could be so many spoons in the whole wide world."

"There is more to this world than anyone could imagine," said a booming voice from the darkness.

"True, true," whispered Roscuro. "The old jailer speaks true."

"Gor," said Mig. "Who said that?" And she turned in the direction of the jailer's voice.

Chapter Thirty-two ∽
beware of the rats

THE CANDLELIGHT on Mig's tray revealed Gregory limping towards her, the thick rope tied around his ankle, his hands outstretched.

"You, Gregory presumes, have brought food for the jailer."

"Gor," said Mig. She took a step backwards.

"Give it here," said Gregory, and he took the tray from Mig and sat down on an overturned kettle that had rolled free from the tower. He balanced the tray on his knees and stared at the covered plate.

"Gregory assumes that today, again, there is no soup."

"Eh?" said Mig.

"Soup!" shouted Gregory.

"Illegal!" shouted Mig back.

"Most foolish," muttered Gregory as he lifted the cover off the plate, "too foolish to be borne, a world without soup." He picked up a drumstick and put the whole of it in his mouth and chewed and swallowed.

"Here," said Mig, staring hard at him, "you forgot the bones."

"Not forgotten. Chewed."

"Gor," said Mig, staring at Gregory with respect. "You eats the bones. You are most ferocious."

Gregory ate another piece of chicken – a wing – bones and all. And then another. Mig watched him admiringly.

"Someday," she said, moved suddenly to tell this man her deepest wish, "I will be a princess."

At this pronouncement, Chiaroscuro, who was still at Mig's side, did a small, deliberate jig of joy; in the light of the one candle his dancing shadow was large and fearsome indeed.

"Gregory sees you," Gregory said to the rat's shadow.

Roscuro ceased his dance. He moved to hide beneath Mig's skirts.

"Eh?" shouted Mig. "What's that?"

"Nothing," said Gregory. "So you aim to be a princess. Well, everyone has a foolish dream. Gregory, for instance, dreams of a world where soup is legal. And that rat, Gregory is sure, has some foolish dream too."

"If only you knew," whispered Roscuro.

"What?" shouted Mig.

Gregory said nothing more. Instead, he reached into his pocket and then held his napkin up to his face and sneezed into it, once, twice, three times.

"Bless you!" shouted Mig. "Bless you, bless you."

"Back to the world of light," Gregory whispered. And then he balled the napkin up and placed it on the tray.

"Gregory is done," he said. And he held the tray out to Mig.

"Done are you? Then the tray goes back upstairs. Cook says it must. You take the tray to the deep downs, you wait for the old man to eat and then you bring the tray back. Them's my instructions."

"Did they instruct you, too, to beware of the rats?"

"The what?"

"The rats."

"What about 'em?"

"Beware of them!" shouted Gregory.

"Right," said Mig. "Beware the rats."

Roscuro, hidden beneath Mig's skirts, rubbed his front paws together. "Warn her all you like, old man," he whispered. "My hour has arrived. The time is now, and your rope must break. No nib-nib-nibbling this time, rather a serious chew that will break it in two. Yes, it is all coming clear. Revenge is at hand."

Chapter Thirty-three
a rat who knows her name

MIG HAD CLIMBED the dungeon stairs and was preparing to open the door to the kitchen, when the rat spoke to her.

"May I detain you for a moment?"

Mig looked to her left and then to her right.

"Down here," said Roscuro.

Mig looked at the floor.

"Gor," she said, "but you're a rat, ain't you? And didn't the old man just warn me of such? 'Beware the rats,' he said." She held the tray up higher so that the light from the candle shone directly on Roscuro and the golden spoon on his head and the blood-red cloak around his neck.

"There is no need to panic, none at all," said Roscuro. As he talked, he reached behind his back and, using the handle, he raised the soup spoon off his head, much in the manner of a man lifting his hat to a lady.

"Gor," said Mig, "a rat with manners."

"Yes," said Roscuro. "How do you do?"

"My papa had him some cloth much like yours, Mr. Rat," said Mig. "Red like that. He traded me for it."

"Ah," said Roscuro, and he smiled a large, knowing smile. "Ah, did he really? That is a terrible story, a tragic story."

Reader, if you will pardon me, we must pause for a moment to consider a great and unusual thing, a portentous thing. That great, unusual, portentous thing is this: Roscuro's voice was pitched perfectly to make its way through the tortuous path of Mig's broken-down, cauliflower ears. That is to say, dear reader, Miggery Sow heard, perfect and true, every single word the rat Roscuro uttered.

"You have known your share of tragedy," said

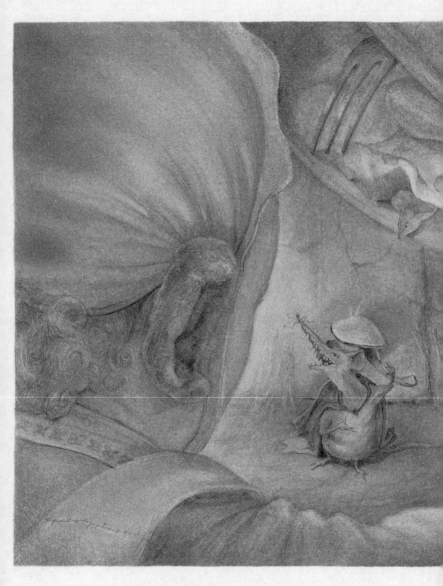

"A rat who knows my name!"

Roscuro to Mig. "Perhaps it is time for you to make the acquaintance of triumph and glory."

"Triumph?" said Mig. "Glory?"

"Allow me to introduce myself," said Roscuro. "I am Chiaroscuro. Friends call me Roscuro. And your name is Miggery Sow. And it is true, is it not, that most people call you simply Mig?"

"Ain't that the thing?" shouted Mig. "A rat who knows my name!"

"Miss Miggery, my dear, I do not want to appear too forward so early in our acquaintance, but, may I enquire, am I right in ascertaining that you have aspirations?"

"What do ye mean 'aspirations'?" shouted Mig.

"Miss Miggery, there is no need to shout. None at all. As you can hear me, so I can hear you. We two are perfectly suited, each to the other." Roscuro smiled again, displaying a mouthful of sharp yellow teeth. "'Aspirations', my dear, are those things that would make a serving girl wish to be a princess."

"Gor," agreed Mig, "a princess is exactly what I want to be."

"There is, my dear, a way to make that happen. I believe that there is a way to make that dream come true."

"You mean that I could be the Princess Pea?"

"Yes, Your Highness," said Roscuro. And he swept the spoon off his head and bowed deeply at the waist. "Yes, your most royal Princess Pea."

"Gor!" said Mig.

"May I tell you my plan? May I illustrate for you how we can make your dream of becoming a princess a reality?"

"Yes," said Mig, "yes."

"It begins," said Roscuro, "with yours truly, and the chewing of a rope."

Mig held the tray with the one small candle burning bright, and she listened as the rat went on, speaking directly to the wish in her heart. So passionately did Roscuro speak and so intently did the serving girl listen that neither noticed as the napkin on the tray moved.

Nor did they hear the small mouselike noises of disbelief and outrage that issued from the napkin as Roscuro went on unfolding, step by step, his diabolical plan to bring the princess to darkness.

Book
THE FOURTH

*Recalled
to the Light*

Chapter Thirty-four
kill 'em, even if they's already dead

READER, you did not forget about our small mouse, did you?

"Back to the light", that was what Gregory whispered to him when he wrapped Despereaux in his napkin and placed him on the tray. And then Mig, after her conversation with Roscuro, carried the tray into the kitchen, and when she saw Cook she shouted, "It's me, Miggery Sow, back from the deep downs."

"Ah, lovely," said Cook. "And ain't we all relieved?"

Mig put the tray on the counter.

"Here, here," said Cook, "your duties ain't done. You must clear it."

"How's that?" shouted Mig.

"You must clear the tray!" shouted Cook. She reached over and took hold of the napkin and gave it a good shake, and Despereaux tumbled out of the napkin and landed right directly, *plop*, in a measuring cup full of oil.

"Acccck," said Cook, "a mouse in my kitchen, in my cooking oil, in my measuring cup. You, Mig, kill him directly."

Mig bent her head and looked at the mouse slowly sinking to the bottom of the glass cup.

"Poor little meecy," she said. And she stuck her hand into the oil and pulled him out by his tail.

Despereaux, gasping and coughing and blinking at the bright light, could have wept with joy at his rescue. But he was not given time to cry.

"Kill him!" shouted Cook.

"Gor!" said Mig. "All right." Holding Despereaux by the tail, she went to get the kitchen knife. But the mouse tail, covered as it was in oil, was slick and difficult to hold onto and Mig, in reaching for the knife, loosened her grip, and Despereaux fell to the floor.

Mig looked down at the little bundle of brown fur.

"Gor," she said, "that killed him for sure."

"Kill him even if he's already dead," shouted Cook. "That's my philosophy with mice. If they're alive, kill them. If they're dead, kill them. That way you can be certain of having yourself a dead mouse, which is the only kind of mouse to have."

"That's some good sophosy, that is, kill 'em, even if they's already dead."

"Hurry, you cauliflower-eared fool!" shouted Cook. "Hurry!"

Despereaux lifted his head from the floor. The afternoon sun was shining through the large kitchen window. He just had time to think how miraculous the light was and then it disappeared and Mig's face loomed into view. She studied him, breathing through her mouth.

"Little meecy," she said, "ain't you going to skedaddle?"

Despereaux looked for a long moment into Mig's

"Gor!" shouted Mig. "Missed him."

small, concerned eyes and then there came a blinding flash and the sound of metal moving through air as Mig brought the kitchen knife down, down, down.

Despereaux felt a very intense pain in his hindquarters. He leapt up and into action. Reader, he scurried. He scurried like a professional mouse. He zigged to the left. He zagged to the right.

"Gor!" shouted Mig. "Missed him."

"Ain't that a surprise?" said Cook just as Despereaux scurried under a crack in the pantry door.

"I got the little meecy's tail, though," said Mig. She bent over and picked up Despereaux's tail and held it up, proudly displaying it to Cook.

"So?" shouted Cook. "What good will that do us when the rest of him has disappeared into the pantry?"

"I don't know," said Mig. And she braced herself as Cook advanced upon her, intending to give her a good clout to the ear. "I don't know."

Chapter Thirty-five
the knight in shining armour

DESPEREAUX WAS PONDERING the
reverse of that question. He was wondering not
what he would do with his tail, but what he would
do without it. He was sitting on a bag of flour high
atop a shelf in the pantry, crying for what he had
lost.

The pain in his hindquarters was intense and
he wept because of it. But he also cried because he
was happy. He was out of the dungeon; he had been
recalled to life. His rescue had happened just in
time for him to save the Princess Pea from the terrible fate that the rat had planned for her.

So Despereaux wept with joy and with pain and with gratitude. He wept with exhaustion and despair and hope. He wept with all the emotions a young, small mouse who has been sent to his death and then been delivered from it in time to save his beloved can feel.

Reader, the mouse wept.

And then he lay down on the sack of flour and slept. Outside the castle the sun set and the stars came out one by one, and then they disappeared and gave way to the rising sun and still Despereaux slept. And while he slept, he dreamt.

He dreamt of the stained-glass windows and the dark of the dungeon. In Despereaux's dream, the light came to life, brilliant and glorious, in the shape of a knight swinging a sword. The knight fought the dark.

And the dark took many shapes. First the dark was his mother, uttering phrases in French. And then the dark became his father beating the drum. The dark was Furlough wearing a black hood and shaking his head no. And the dark became a huge rat smiling a smile that was evil and sharp.

"The dark," Despereaux cried, turning his head to the left.

"The light," he murmured, turning his head to the right.

He called out to the knight. He shouted, "Who are you? Will you save me?"

But the knight did not answer him.

"Tell me who you are!" Despereaux shouted.

The knight stopped swinging his sword. He looked at Despereaux. "You know me," he said.

"No," said Despereaux, "I don't."

"You do," said the knight. He slowly took the armour off his head and revealed … nothing, no one. The suit of armour was empty.

"No, oh no," said Despereaux. "There is no knight in shining armour; it's all just make-believe, like happily ever after."

And in his sleep, reader, the small mouse began to cry.

Chapter Thirty-six ~
what Mig carried

AND WHILE THE MOUSE SLEPT, Roscuro put his terrible plan into effect. Would you like to hear, reader, how it all unfolded? The story is not a pretty one. There is violence in it. And cruelty. But stories that are not pretty have a certain value, too, I suppose. Everything, as you well know (having lived in this world long enough to have figured out a thing or two for yourself), cannot always be sweetness and light.

Listen. This is how it happened. First, the rat finished, once and for all, the job he had started long ago: He chewed through Gregory's rope, all the way through it, so that the jailer became lost in the maze of the dungeon. Late at night, when the castle was dark, the serving girl Miggery Sow climbed the stairs to the princess's room.

In her hand she carried a candle. And in the pockets of her apron were two very ominous things. In the right pocket, hidden in case they should encounter anyone on the stairs, was a rat with a spoon on his head and a cloak of red around his shoulders. In the left pocket was a kitchen knife, the same knife that Miggery Sow had used to cut off the tail of a certain mouse. These were the things, a rat and a knife and a candle, that Mig carried with her as she climbed up, up, up the stairs.

"Gor!" she shouted to the rat. "It's dark, ain't it?"

"Yes, yes," whispered Roscuro from her pocket. "It is quite dark, my dear."

"When I'm princess—" began Mig.

"Shhhh," said Roscuro, "may I suggest that you keep your glorious plans for the future to yourself? And may I further suggest that you keep your voice down to a whisper? We are, after all, on a covert mission. Do you know how to whisper, my dear?"

"I do!" shouted Mig.

"Then, please," said Roscuro, "please institute this knowledge immediately."

"Gor," whispered Mig, "all right."

"Thank you," said Roscuro. "Do I need to review with you again our plan of action?"

"I got it all straight right here in my head," whispered Mig. And she tapped the side of her head with one finger.

"How comforting," said Roscuro. "Perhaps, my dear, we should go over it again. One more time, just to be sure."

"Well," said Mig, "we go into the princess's room and she will be sleeping and snoozing and snoring, and I will wake her up and show her the knife and say, 'If you does not want to get hurt, Princess, you must come with me.'"

"And you will not hurt her," said Roscuro.

"No, I won't. Because I want her to live so that she can be my lady-in-waiting when I become the princess."

"Exactly," said Roscuro. "That will be her divine comeuppance."

"Gor," whispered Mig. "Yes. Her divine come-uppance."

Mig had, of course, no idea what the phrase "divine comeuppance" meant, but she very much liked the sound of it, and she repeated it over and over to herself until Roscuro said, "And then?"

"And then," continued Mig, "I tells her to get out of her princess bed and come with me on a little journey."

"Ha," said Roscuro, "a little journey. That is right. Ha. I love the understatement of that phrase. A little journey. Oh, it will be a little journey. Indeed, it will."

"And then," said Mig, who was now coming to her favourite part of the plan, "we take her to the deep downs and we gives her some long lessons in how to be a serving girl and we gives me some short lessons in how to be a princess and when we is all done studying up, we switch places. I gets to be the princess and she gets to be the maid. Gor!"

Reader, this is the very plan that Roscuro presented to Mig when he first met her. It was, of course, a ridiculous plan.

No one would ever, not for one blind minute, mistake Mig for the princess or the princess for Mig. But Miggery Sow, as I pointed out to you before, was not the sharpest knife in the drawer. And, reader, too, she wanted so desperately to become a princess. She wanted – oh, how she wanted. And it was because of this terrible wanting that she was able to believe in Roscuro's plan with every ounce of her heart.

The rat's real plan was, in a way, more simple and more terrible. He intended to take the princess to the deepest, darkest part of the dungeon. He intended to have Mig put chains on the princess's hands and her feet, and he intended to keep the glittering, glowing, laughing princess there in the dark.

For ever.

Chapter Thirty-seven
a small taste

SHE WAS ASLEEP and dreaming of her mother, the queen, who was holding out a spoon to her and saying, "Taste this, my sweet Pea, taste this, my darling, and tell me what you think."

The princess leant forward and sipped some soup from the spoon her mother held out to her.

"Oh, Mama," she said, "it's wonderful. It's the best soup I have ever eaten."

"Yes," said the queen. "It is wonderful, isn't it?"

"May I have some more?" said the Pea.

"I gave you a small taste so that you would not forget," said her mother. "I gave you a small taste so that you would remember."

"I want more."

But as soon as the princess said this, her mother was gone. She disappeared and the bowl and the soup spoon disappeared along with her.

"Lost things," said the Pea, "more lost things." And then she heard her name. She turned, happy, thinking that her mother had come back. But the voice was not her mother's. The voice belonged to somebody else and it was coming from some place far away and it was telling her to wake up, wake up.

The Pea opened her eyes and saw Miggery Sow standing over her bed, a knife in one hand and a candle in the other.

"Mig?" she said.

"Gor," said Mig softly.

"Say it," commanded Roscuro.

Mig closed her eyes and shouted her piece. "If you does not want to get hurt, Princess, you must come with me."

"Whatever for?" said the princess in an annoyed tone. As I have noted before, the princess was not a person who was used to being told what to do.

"What are you talking about?"

Mig opened her eyes and shouted, "You got to come with me so after we take some lessons, you some long lessons and me some short ones, together way down in the deep downs, I can be you and you can be me."

"No!" shouted Roscuro from Mig's pocket. "No! No! You are doing it wrong."

"Who said that?"

"Your Highness," said Roscuro. And he crawled out of Mig's pocket and made his way up to her shoulder and situated himself there, laying his tail across her neck to balance himself. "Your Highness," he said again. And he raised the spoon slowly off his head and smiled, displaying his mouthful of truly hideous teeth. "I think it would be best if you do as Miggery Sow suggests. She is, as you can quite clearly see, in possession of a knife, a large knife. And she will, if pushed, use it."

"This is ridiculous," the princess said. "You can't threaten me. I'm a princess."

"We," said Roscuro, "are all too aware of the fact of what you are. A knife, however, cares nothing for the fact that you are royalty. And you will bleed, I assume, just like any other human."

The Pea looked at Mig. Mig smiled. The knife glinted in the light of the candle. "Mig?" she said, her voice shaking the tiniest bit.

"I really do not think," said Roscuro, "that Mig would need much persuasion to use that knife, Princess. She is a dangerous individual, easily led."

"But we are friends," said the Pea, "aren't we, Mig?"

"Eh?" said Mig.

"Trust me," said Roscuro. "You are not friends. And I think it would be best if you addressed all your communications to me, Princess. I am the one in charge here. Look at me."

The Pea looked right directly at the rat and at the spoon on his head. Her heart skipped one beat and then two.

"Do you know me, Princess?"

"No," she said, lowering her head, "I don't know you."

But, reader, she did know him. He was the rat who had fallen in her mother's soup. And he was wearing her dead mother's spoon on his head! The

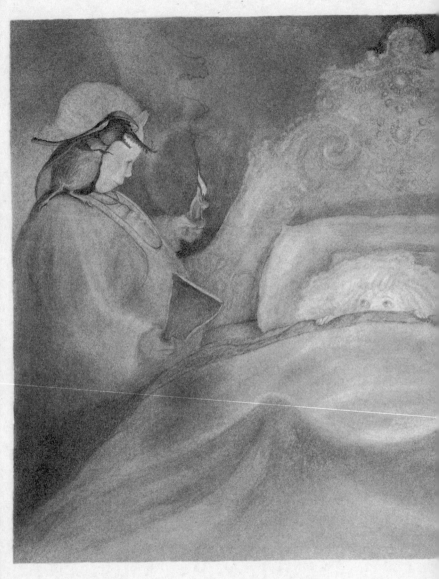

"Do you know me, Princess?"

princess kept her head down. She concentrated on containing the rage that was leaping up inside of her.

"Look again, Princess. Or can you not bear to look? Does it pain your royal sensibilities to let your eyes rest on a *rat*?"

"I don't know you," she said, "and I'm not afraid to look at you." The Pea raised her head slowly. Her eyes were defiant. She stared at the rat.

"Very well," said Roscuro, "have it your way. You do not know me. Nonetheless, you must do as I say, as my friend here has a knife. So get out of bed, Princess. We are going on a little journey. I would like it if you dressed in your loveliest gown, the one that you were wearing at a banquet not so long ago."

"And put on your crown," said Mig. "Put that on your princess head."

"Yes," said Roscuro. "Please, Princess, do not forget your crown."

The Pea, still staring at Roscuro, pushed the covers back and got out of bed.

"Move quickly," said Roscuro. "We must take our little journey while it is still dark and while the rest of the castle sleeps on – ignorant, oh so ignorant, I am afraid, of your fate."

The princess took a gown from her closet.

"Yes," said Roscuro to himself, "that is the one. The very one. Look at how it sparkles in the light. Lovely."

"I will need someone to do my buttons," said the princess as she stepped into the dress. "Mig, you must help me."

"Little princess," said Roscuro, "do you think that you can outsmart a rat? Our dear Miggery Sow will not lay down her knife. Not even for a moment. Will you, Miggery Sow? Because that might ruin your chances of becoming a princess, isn't that right?"

"Gor," said Mig, "that's right."

And so while Mig held the knife pointed in the direction of the princess, the Pea sat and let the rat crawl over her back, doing her buttons up for her, one by one.

The princess held very still. The only movement she allowed herself was this: she licked her lips, over and over again, because she thought that she could taste there the sweet saltiness of the soup that her mother had fed her in her dream.

"I have not forgotten, Mama," she whispered. "I have not forgotten you. I have not forgotten soup."

Chapter Thirty-eight
to the dungeon

THE STRANGE THREESOME made their way down the golden stairs of the castle. The princess and Mig walked side by side and Roscuro hid himself again in the pocket of Mig's apron, and Mig pointed the sharp tip of the knife at the princess's back and together they went down, down, down.

The princess was led to her fate as, around her, everyone slept. The king slept in his giant bed with his crown on his head and his hands crossed on his chest, dreaming that his wife, the queen, was a bird with green and gold feathers who called his name, *Phillip, Phillip, Phillip*, without ceasing.

Cook slept in a too-small bed off the kitchen, dreaming of a recipe for soup that she could not find. "Where did I put that?" she mumbled in her sleep. "Where did that recipe go? It was for the queen's favourite soup. I must find it."

And not far from Cook, in the pantry, atop a bag of flour, slept the mouse Despereaux, dreaming, as you know, reader, of knights in shining armour, of darkness, and of light.

And in the whole of the darkened, sleeping castle, there was only the light of the candle in the hand of Miggery Sow. The candle shone on the princess's dress and made it sparkle, and the princess walked tall in the light and tried not to be afraid.

In this story, reader, we have talked about the heart of the mouse and the heart of the rat and the heart of the serving girl Miggery Sow, but we have not talked about the heart of the princess. Like most hearts, it was complicated, shaded with dark and dappled with light. The dark things in the princess's heart were these: a very small, very hot, burning coal of hatred for the rat who was responsible for her mother's death. And the other darkness was a tremendous sorrow, a deep sadness that her mother was dead and that the princess could, now, only talk to her in her dreams.

And what of the light in the princess's heart? Reader, I am pleased to tell you that the Pea was a kind person, and perhaps more importantly, she was empathetic. Do you know what it means to be empathetic?

I will tell you: It means that when you are being forcibly taken to a dungeon, when you have a large knife pointed at your back, when you are trying to be brave, you are able, still, to think for a moment of the person who is holding that knife.

You are able to think: "Oh, poor Mig, she wants to be a princess so badly and she thinks that this is the way. Poor, poor Mig. What must it be like to want something that desperately?"

That, reader, is empathy.

And now you have a small map of the princess's heart (hatred, sorrow, kindness, empathy), the heart that she carried inside her as she went down the golden stairs and through the kitchen and, finally, just as the sky outside the castle began to lighten, down into the dark of the dungeon with the rat and the serving girl.

Chapter Thirty-nine ⌒
missing!

THE SUN ROSE AND SHED LIGHT
on what Roscuro and Miggery Sow had done.

And finally Despereaux awoke. But, alas, he awoke too late.

"I haven't seen her," Louise was shouting, "and I tell you, I wash my hands of her. If she's missing, I say good riddance! Good riddance to bad rubbish."

Despereaux sat up. He looked behind him. Oh, his tail! Gone! Given over to the knife, and where the tail should be ... nothing but a bloody stub.

"And more foul play. Gregory dead!" shouted Cook. "Poor old man, that rope of his broken by who knows what and him lost in the dark and frightened to death because of it. It's too much."

"Oh no," whispered Despereaux. "Oh no, Gregory is dead." The mouse got to his feet and began the long climb down from the shelf. Once he was on the floor, he stuck his head around the door of the pantry and saw Cook standing in the centre of the kitchen, wringing her fat hands. Beside her stood a tall woman jangling a ring of keys.

"That's right," said Louise. "All the king's men was down there searching for her in the dungeon and when they come back up, who do they have with them? They have the old man. Dead! And now you tell me that Mig is missing and I say who cares?"

Despereaux made a small noise of despair. He had slept too long. The rat had already acted. The princess was gone.

"What kind of world is it, Miss Louise, where princesses are taken from right under our noses and queens drop dead and we cannot even take comfort in soup?" And with this, Cook started to cry.

"Shhhh," said Louise, "I beg you. Do not say that word."

"Soup!" shouted Cook. "I will say it. No one can stop me. Soup, soup, *soup!*" And then she began to cry in earnest, wailing and sobbing.

"There," said Louise. She put a hand out to touch Cook, and Cook slapped it away.

"It will be all right," said Louise.

Cook brought the hem of her apron up to wipe at her tears. "It won't," she said. "It won't be all right ever again. They've taken our little darling away. There ain't nothing left to live for without the princess."

Despereaux was amazed to have exactly what was in his heart spoken aloud by such a ferocious, mouse-hating woman as Cook.

Louise again reached out to touch Cook, and this time Cook allowed her to put an arm around her shoulder. "What will we do? What will we do?" wailed Cook.

And Louise said, "Shhh. There, there."

Alas, there was no one to comfort Despereaux. And there was no time, anyway, for him to cry. He knew what he had to do. He had to find the king.

For, having heard Roscuro's plan, reader,

Despereaux knew that the princess was hidden in the dungeon. And being somewhat smarter than Miggery Sow, he sensed the terrible unspoken truth behind Roscuro's words. He knew that Mig could never be a princess. And he knew that the rat, once he captured the Pea, would never let her go.

And so, the small mouse who had been dipped in oil, covered in flour and relieved of his tail slipped out of the pantry and past the weeping ladies.

He went to find the king.

Chapter Forty
forgiveness

HE WENT FIRST to the throne room, but the king was not there. And so Despereaux slipped through a hole in the moulding, and was making his way to the princess's room when he came upon the Mouse Council, thirteen mice and one Most Very Honoured Head Mouse, sitting around their piece of wood debating important mouse matters.

Despereaux stopped and stood very still.

"Fellow honoured mice," said the Most Very Honoured Head Mouse, and then he looked up from the makeshift table and saw Despereaux. "Despereaux," he whispered.

The other mice of the council leaned forward, straining to make some sense of the word that the Head Mouse had just uttered.

"Pardon?" one said.

"Excuse me?" said another.

"I didn't hear right," said a third. "I thought you said 'Despereaux'."

The Head Mouse gathered himself. He tried speaking again. "Fellow members," he said, "a ghost. A ghost!" And he raised a shaking paw and pointed it at Despereaux.

The other mice turned and looked.

And there was Despereaux Tilling, covered in flour, looking back at them, the telltale red thread still around his neck like a thin trail of blood.

"Despereaux," said Lester. "Son. You have come back!"

Despereaux looked at his father and saw an old mouse whose fur was shot through with grey. How could that be? Despereaux had been gone only a few days, but his father seemed to have aged many years in his absence.

"Son, ghost of my son," said Lester, his whiskers

"Son. You have come back!"

trembling, "I dream about you every night. I dream about beating the drum that sent you to your death. I was wrong. What I did was wrong."

"No!" called the Most Very Honoured Head Mouse. "No!"

"I've destroyed it," said Lester. "I've destroyed the drum. Will you forgive me?" He clasped his front paws together and looked at his son.

"No!" shouted the Head Mouse again. "No. Do not ask the ghost to forgive you, Lester. You did as you should. You did what was best for the mouse community."

Lester ignored the Head Mouse. "Son," he said, "please."

Despereaux looked at his father, at his grey-streaked fur and trembling whiskers and his front paws clasped together in front of his heart, and he felt suddenly as if his own heart would break in two. His father looked so small, so sad.

"Forgive me," said Lester again.

Forgiveness, reader, is, I think, something very much like hope and love – a powerful, wonderful thing.

And a ridiculous thing, too.

Isn't it ridiculous, after all, to think that a son could forgive his father for beating the drum that sent him to his death? Isn't it ridiculous to think that a mouse could ever forgive anyone for such perfidy?

But still, here are the words Despereaux Tilling spoke to his father. He said, "I forgive you, Pa."

And he said those words because he sensed that it was the only way to save his own heart, to stop it from breaking in two. Despereaux, reader, spoke those words to save himself.

And then he turned from his father and spoke to the whole Mouse Council. "You were wrong," he said. "All of you. You asked me to renounce my sins; I ask you to renounce yours. You wronged me. Repent."

"Never," said the Head Mouse.

Despereaux stood before the Mouse Council and he realized that he was a different mouse from the one who had faced them the last time. He had been to the dungeon and back up out of it. He knew things that they would never know; what they thought of him, he realized, did not matter, not at all.

And so, without saying another word, Despereaux turned and left the room.

After he had gone, the Head Mouse slapped his trembling paw on the table. "Mice of the Council," he said, "we have been paid a visit by a ghost who has told us to repent. We will now take a vote. All in favour of saying that this visit did *not* occur, vote 'aye'."

And from the members of the Mouse Council there came a tiny but emphatic chorus of "ayes".

Only one mouse said nothing. That mouse was Despereaux's father. Lester Tilling had turned his head away from the other members of the Mouse Council; he was trying to hide his tears.

He was crying, reader, because he had been forgiven.

Chapter Forty-one
the tears of a king

DESPEREAUX FOUND THE KING in the Pea's room, sitting on his daughter's bed, clutching the tapestry of her life to his chest. He was weeping. Although "weeping", really, is too small a word for the activity that the king had undertaken. Tears were cascading from his eyes. A small puddle had formed at his feet. I am not exaggerating. The king, it seemed, was intent on crying himself a river.

Reader, have you ever seen a king cry? When the powerful are made weak, when they are revealed to be human, to have hearts, their diminishment is nothing short of terrifying.

You can be sure that Despereaux was terrified. Absolutely. But he spoke up anyway.

"Sir?" the mouse said to the king.

But the king did not hear him, and as Despereaux watched, King Phillip dropped the tapestry and took his great golden crown from his lap and used it to beat himself on the chest over and over again. The king, as I have already mentioned, had several faults. He was near-sighted. He made ridiculous, unreasonable, difficult-to-enforce laws. And, much in the way of Miggery Sow, he was not exactly the sharpest knife in the drawer.

But there was one extraordinary, wonderful, admirable thing about the king. He was a man who was able and willing to love with the whole of his heart. And just as he had loved the queen with the whole of his heart, so, too, he loved his daughter with the whole of it, even more than the whole. He loved the Princess Pea with every particle of his being, and she had been taken from him.

But what Despereaux had come to say to the king had to be said, and so he tried again. "Excuse me," he said. He wasn't certain, really, how a mouse should address a king. "Sir" did not seem like a big enough word. Despereaux thought about it for a long moment.

He cleared his throat. He spoke as loudly as he was capable of speaking. "Excuse me, Most Very Honoured Head Person."

King Phillip stopped beating his crown against his chest. He looked around the room.

"Down here, Most Very Honoured Head Person," said Despereaux.

The king, tears still falling from his eyes, looked at the floor. He squinted.

"Is that a bug speaking to me?" he asked.

"No," said Despereaux, "I am a mouse. We met before."

"A mouse!" bellowed the king. "A mouse is but one step removed from a rat."

"Sir," said Despereaux, "Most Very Honoured Head Person, please, you have to listen to me. This is important. I know where your daughter is."

"You do?" said the king. He sniffed. He blew his nose on his royal cloak. "Where?" he said, and as he bent over to look more closely at Despereaux, one tear, two tears, three enormous, king-sized tears fell with an audible *plop* onto Despereaux's head and rolled down his back, washing away the white of the flour and revealing his own brown fur.

"Sir, Most Very Honoured Head Person, sir," said Despereaux as he wiped the king's tears out of his own eyes, "she's in the dungeon."

"Liar," said the king. He sat back up. "I knew it. All rodents are liars and thieves. She is not in the dungeon. My men have searched the dungeon."

"But no one really knows the dungeon except the rats, sir. There are thousands of places where she could be hidden, and only the rats would know. Your men would never be able to find her if the rats did not want her found."

"Accccck," said the king, and he clapped his hands over his ears. "Do not speak to me of rats and what they know!" he shouted. "Rats are illegal. Rats are against the law. There are no rats in my kingdom. They do not exist."

"Sir, Most Very Honoured Head Person, that is not true. Hundreds of rats live in the dungeon of this castle. One of them has taken your daughter, and if you will send—"

The king started humming. "I can't hear you!" he stopped to shout. "I cannot hear you! And anyway, what you say is wrong because you are a rodent and therefore a liar." He started to hum again. And then he stopped and said, "I have hired fortune-tellers. And a magician. They are coming from a distant land. They will tell me where my beautiful daughter is. They will speak the truth. A mouse cannot speak the truth."

"I am telling you the truth," said Despereaux. "I promise."

But the king would not listen. He sat with his hands over his ears. He hummed loudly. Big fat tears rolled down his face and fell to the floor.

Despereaux sat and stared at him in dismay. What should he do now? He put a nervous paw up to his neck and pulled at the red thread, and suddenly his dream came flooding back to him … the dark and the light and the knight swinging his sword and the terrible moment when he had realized that the suit of armour was empty.

And then, reader, as he stood before the king, a wonderful, amazing thought occurred to the mouse. What if the suit of armour had been empty for a reason? What if it had been empty because it was waiting?

For him.

"You know me" – that was what the knight in his dream had said.

"Yes," said Despereaux out loud in wonder. "I do know you."

"I can't hear you," sang the king.

"I'll have to do it myself," said the mouse. "I will be the knight in shining armour. There is no other way. It has to be me."

Despereaux turned. He left the weeping king. He went to find the threadmaster.

Chapter Forty-two
the rest of the thread

THE THREADMASTER was sitting atop his spool of thread, swinging his tail back and forth and eating a piece of celery.

"Well, look here," he said when he saw Despereaux. "Would you just look at that. It's the mouse who loved a human princess, back from the dungeon in one piece. The old threadmaster would say that I didn't do my job well, that because you are still alive I must have tied the thread incorrectly. But it is not so. And how do I know it is not so? Because the thread is still around your neck." He nodded and took a bite of his celery.

"I need the rest of it," said Despereaux.

"The rest of what? Your neck?"

"The rest of the thread."

"Well, I can't just hand it over to any old mouse," said the threadmaster. "They say red thread is special, sacred; though I, myself, after having spent so much time with it, know it for what it is."

"What is it?" said Despereaux.

"Thread," said the threadmaster. He shrugged and took another loud bite of celery. "Nothing more. Nothing less. But I pretend, friend, I pretend. And what, may I ask, do you intend to do with the thread?"

"Save the princess."

"Ah, yes, the princess. The beautiful princess. That's how this whole story started, isn't it?"

"I have to save her. There is no one but me to do it."

"It seems to be that way with most things. No one to do the really disagreeable jobs except oneself. And how, exactly, will you use a spool of thread to save a princess?"

"A rat has taken her and hidden her in the

dungeon, so I have to go back to the dungeon, and it is full of twists and turns and hidden chambers."

"Like a maze," said the threadmaster.

"Yes, like a maze. And I have to find my way to her, wherever she is hidden, and then I have to lead her back out again, and the only way to do that is with the thread. Gregory the jailer tied a rope around his ankle so that he would not get lost." As the mouse said this he shuddered, thinking of Gregory and his broken rope, dying, lost in the darkness. "I," said Despereaux, "I ... will use thread."

The threadmaster nodded. "I see, I see," he said. He took a meditative bite of celery. "You, friend, are on a quest."

"I don't know what that is," said Despereaux.

"You don't have to know. You just have to feel compelled to do the thing: the impossible, important task at hand."

"Impossible?" said Despereaux.

"Impossible," said the threadmaster. "Important." He sat chewing his celery and staring somewhere past Despereaux, and then suddenly he leapt off his spool.

"Who am I to stand in the way of a quest?" he said. "Roll her away."

"I can have it?"

"Yes. For your quest."

Despereaux put his front paws up and touched the spool. He gave it an experimental push forward.

"Thank you," he said, looking into the eye of the threadmaster. "I don't know your name."

"Hovis."

"Thank you, Hovis."

"There's something else. Something that belongs with the thread." Hovis went into a corner and came back with a needle. "You can use it for protection."

"Like a sword," said Despereaux. "Like a knight would have."

"Yes," said Hovis. He gnawed off a length of thread and used it to tie the needle around Despereaux's waist. "Like so."

"Thank you, Hovis," said Despereaux. He put his right shoulder against the spool of thread and pushed it forward again.

"Wait," said Hovis. He stood up on his hind legs,

"You see, you're not going into the dungeon because you
have to. You're going because you choose to."

put his paws on Despereaux's shoulders, and leaned in close to him. Despereaux smelt the sharp, clean scent of celery as the threadmaster bent his head, took hold of the thread around Despereaux's neck in his sharp teeth, and pulled on it hard.

"There," said Hovis, when the piece of thread broke and dropped to the ground. "Now you're free. You see, you're not going into the dungeon because you have to. You're going because you choose to."

"Yes," said Despereaux, "because I am on a quest." The word felt good and right in his mouth. *Quest.*

Say it, reader. Say the word "quest" out loud. It is an extraordinary word, is it not? So small and yet so full of wonder, so full of hope.

"Goodbye," said Hovis as Despereaux pushed the spool of thread out of the threadmaster's hole. "I have never known a mouse who has made it out of the dungeon only to go back into it again. Goodbye, friend. Goodbye, mouse among mice."

Chapter Forty-three *what Cook was stirring*

THAT NIGHT Despereaux rolled the thread from the threadmaster's lair, along innumerable hallways and down three flights of stairs.

Reader, allow me to put this in perspective for you: Your average house mouse (or castle mouse, if you will) weighs somewhere in the neighbourhood of four ounces.

Despereaux, as you well know, was in no way average. In fact, he was so incredibly small that he weighed about half of what the average mouse weighs: two ounces. That is all. Think about it: He was nothing but two ounces of mouse pushing a spool of thread that weighed almost as much as he did.

Honestly, reader, what do you think the chances are of such a small mouse succeeding in his quest?

Zip. Zero. Nil.

None whatsoever.

But you must, when you are calculating the odds of the mouse's success, factor in his love for the princess. Love, as we have already discussed, is a powerful, wonderful, ridiculous thing, capable of moving mountains. And spools of thread.

Even with the love and purpose in his heart, however, Despereaux was very, very tired when he reached the door to the castle kitchen at midnight. His paws were shaking and his muscles were jumping and the place where his tail should be was throbbing. And he still had a very, very long way to go, into the kitchen and down the many stairs of the dungeon, and then through, somehow, some way, *through* the rat-filled darkness of the dungeon itself, not knowing where he was going ... and oh, reader, when he stopped to consider what lay ahead of him Despereaux was filled with a nasty feeling of despair.

He leant his head against the spool of thread, and he smelt celery there and he thought of Hovis and how Hovis seemed to believe in him and his quest. So the mouse raised his head and squared his shoulders and pushed the spool of thread forward again, into the kitchen, where he saw, too late, that there was a light burning.

Despereaux froze.

Cook was in the kitchen. She was bent over the stove. She was stirring something.

Was it a sauce? No.

Was it a stew? No.

What Cook was stirring was ... soup. Soup, reader! In the king's own castle, against the king's law, right under the king's very nose, Cook was making soup!

As the mouse looked on, Cook put her face into the steam rising from the pot and took a deep breath. She smiled a beatific smile, and the steam rose around her and caught the light of the candle and made a halo over her head.

Despereaux knew how Cook felt about mice in her kitchen. He remembered quite clearly her instructions to Mig regarding himself: Kill him. The only good mouse is a dead mouse.

But he had to go through Cook's kitchen to get to the dungeon door. And he had no time to waste. Soon daylight would dawn and the whole castle would be awake and a mouse would have no chance at all of pushing a spool of thread across the floor without attracting a great deal of attention. He would have to sneak past the mouse-hating Cook now.

And so, screwing his courage to the sticking place, Despereaux leant against the spool of thread and set it rolling across the floor.

Cook turned from the stove, a dripping spoon in her hand and a frightened look on her face, and shouted, "Who's there?"

Chapter Forty-four
whose ears are those?

"WHO'S THERE?" shouted Cook again.

Despereaux, wisely, said nothing.

The kitchen was silent.

"Hmmmmph," said Cook. "Nothing. It's nothing at all. Just my nervous Nellie ears playing tricks on me. You're an old fool," she said to herself as she turned back to the stove. "You're just an old fool afraid of being caught making soup."

Despereaux slumped against the spool of thread. And as he leant there, his heart pounding, his paws shaking, a small wonderful something occurred. A midnight breeze entered the kitchen and danced over to the stove and picked up the scent of the soup and then swirled across the floor and delivered the smell right directly to the mouse's nose.

Despereaux put his head up in the air. He sniffed. He sniffed some more. He had never in his life smelt anything so lovely, so inspiring. With each sniff he took, he felt himself growing stronger, braver.

Cook leant in close to the kettle and put the spoon in and took the spoon out and blew upon the spoon and then brought it to her lips and sipped and swallowed.

"Hmmmmm," she said. "Huh." She took another sip. "Missing something," she said. "More salt, maybe." She put the spoon down and took up an enormous salt shaker and sprinkled salt into the kettle.

And Despereaux, feeling emboldened by the smell of soup, again set to work pushing the spool of thread.

"Quickly," he said to himself, rolling the spool across the floor, "do it quickly. Do not think. Just push."

Cook whirled, the salt shaker in her hand, and shouted, "Who goes there?"

Despereaux stopped pushing. He hid behind the spool of thread as Cook took the candle from the stove and held it up high.

"Hmmmmmph," she said.

The candlelight came closer, closer.

"What's this?"

The light came to rest directly on Despereaux's big ears sticking up from behind the spool of thread.

"Ho," said Cook, "whose ears are those?"

And the light from the candle then shone full in Despereaux's face.

"A mouse," said Cook. "A mouse in my kitchen."

Despereaux closed his eyes. He prepared for his death.

He waited, reader. And waited. And then he heard the sound of laughter.

He opened his eyes and looked at Cook.

"Ho," said Cook. "Ho-hee. For the first time in my life, I am glad to see a mouse in my kitchen.

"Why," she asked, "why am I glad? Ho-hee. Because a mouse is not a king's man here to punish me for making soup. That is why. Because a mouse is not a king's man here to take me to the dungeon for owning a spoon. Ho-hee. A mouse. I, Cook, am glad to see a mouse."

Cook's face was red and her stomach was shaking. "Ho-hee," she said again. "And not just any mouse. A mouse with a needle tied around his waist, a mouse with no tail. Ain't it lovely? Ho-hee." She shook her head and wiped at her eyes. "Look, mouse, these are extraordinary times. And because of that, we must have some peace between us. I will not ask what you are doing in my kitchen. And you, in return, will tell no one what I am cooking."

She turned then and went back to the stove and set down the candle and picked up the spoon and again put it in the pot of soup and took it back out and tasted the soup, smacking her lips together.

"Not right," she said, "not quite right. Missing something, still."

Despereaux did not move. He could not move. He was paralysed by fear. He sat on the kitchen floor. One small tear fell out of his left eye. He had expected Cook to kill him.

Instead, reader, she had laughed at him.

And he was surprised how much her laughter hurt.

Chapter Forty-five
some soup

COOK STIRRED THE SOUP and then put the spoon down and held up the candle and looked over at Despereaux.

"What are you waiting for?" she said. "Go, go, go. There will never be another opportunity for a mouse to escape from my kitchen unharmed."

The smell of soup again wafted in Despereaux's direction. He put his nose up in the air. His whiskers trembled.

"Yes," said Cook. "That is soup that you are smelling. The princess, not that you would know or care, is missing, bless her goodhearted self. And times are terrible. And when times are terrible, soup is the answer. Don't it smell like the answer?"

"Yes," said Despereaux. He nodded.

Cook turned away from him. She put the candle down and picked up her spoon and started to stir. "Oh," she said, "these are dark days." She shook her head. "And I'm kidding myself. There ain't no point in making soup unless others eat it. Soup needs another mouth to taste it, another heart to be warmed by it."

She stopped stirring. She turned and looked at Despereaux.

"Mouse," said Cook, "would you like some soup?" And then, without waiting for an answer, she took a saucer and spooned some soup into it and set it on the kitchen floor.

"Come closer," she said. "I don't aim to hurt you. I promise."

Despereaux sniffed. The soup smelt wonderful, incredible. Keeping one eye on Cook, he stepped out from behind the spool of thread and crept closer.

"Go on," said Cook, "taste it."

Despereaux stepped onto the saucer. Soup

covered his paws. He bent his head to the hot broth. He sipped. Oh, it was lovely. Garlic and chicken and watercress, the same soup that Cook had made the day the queen died.

"How is it?" asked Cook anxiously.

"Wonderful," said Despereaux.

"Too much garlic?" said Cook, wringing her fat hands.

"No," said Despereaux. "It's perfect."

Cook smiled. "See?" she said. "There ain't a body, be it mouse or man, that ain't made better by a little soup."

Despereaux bent his head and sipped again, and Cook stood over him and smiled, saying, "It don't need a thing, then? Is that what you're saying? It's just right?"

Despereaux nodded.

He drank the soup in big, noisy gulps. And when he stepped out of the saucer, his paws were damp and his whiskers were dripping and his stomach was full.

Cook said to him, "Not done already, are you? Surely you ain't done. You must want more."

"It's perfect," he said.

"I can't," said Despereaux. "I don't have time. I'm on my way to the dungeon to save the princess."

"Ho-hee." Cook laughed. "You, a mouse, are going to save the princess?"

"Yes," said Despereaux, "I'm on a quest."

"Well, don't let me stand in your way."

And so it was that Cook held open the door to the dungeon while Despereaux rolled the spool of thread through it. "Good luck," she said to him. "Ho-hee, good luck saving the princess."

She closed the door behind her and then leant against it and shook her head. "And if that ain't an indicator of what strange days these are," she said to herself, "then I don't know what is. Me. Cook. Feeding a mouse soup and then wishing him good luck in saving the princess. Oh my. Strange days indeed."

Chapter Forty-six ∂‿
mouse blood, yes

DESPEREAUX STOOD at the top of the dungeon stairs and peered into the darkness that waited for him below.

"Oh," he said, "oh my."

He had forgotten how dark the dark of the dungeon could be. And he had forgotten, too, its terrible smell, the stench of rats, the odour of suffering.

But his heart was full of love for the princess and his stomach was full of Cook's soup and Despereaux felt brave and strong. And so he began, immediately and without despair, the hard work of manoeuvring the spool of thread down the narrow dungeon steps.

Down, down, down went Despereaux Tilling and the spool of thread. Slowly, oh so slowly, they went. And the passage was dark, dark, dark.

"I will tell myself a story," said Despereaux. "I will make some light. Let's see. It will begin this way: Once upon a time. Yes. Once upon a time, there was a mouse who was very, very small. Exceptionally small. And there was a beautiful human princess whose name was Pea. And it so happened that this mouse was the one who was selected by fate to serve the princess, to honour her and to save her from the darkness of a terrible dungeon."

This story cheered up Despereaux considerably. His eyes became accustomed to the gloom, and he moved down the stairs more quickly, more surely, whispering to himself the tale of a devious rat and a fat serving girl and a beautiful princess and a brave mouse and some soup and a spool of red thread. It was a story, in fact, very similar to the one you are reading right now, and the telling of it gave Despereaux strength.

He pushed the spool of thread with a great deal of gusto. And the thread, eager, perhaps, to begin its honourable task of aiding in the rescue of a princess, leapt forward and away from the mouse and went down the dungeon stairs ahead of him, without him.

"No," cried Despereaux, "no, no, no!" He broke into a trot, chasing the thread through the darkness.

But the spool had a head start. And it was faster. It flew down the dungeon stairs, leaving Despereaux far behind. When it came to the end of the stairs, it rolled and rolled, until finally, lazily, it came to a stop right at the gnarled paw of a rat.

"What have we here?" said the one-eared rat to the spool of thread.

"I will tell you what we have," said Botticelli Remorso, answering his own question. "We have red thread. How delightful. Red thread means one thing to a rat."

He put his nose up in the air. He sniffed. He sniffed again. "I smell … could it be? Yes, most definitely it is. Soup. How strange." He sniffed some more. "And I smell tears. Human tears. Delightful. And I also detect the smell" – he put his nose high into the air and took a big whiff – "of flour and oil. Oh my, what a cornucopia of scents. But below it all, what do I smell? The blood of a mouse. Unmistakably, mouse blood, yes. Ha-ha-ha! Exactly! Mouse."

Botticelli looked down at the spool of thread and smiled. He gave it a gentle push with one paw.

"Red thread. Yes. Exactly. Just when you think that life in the dungeon cannot get any better, a mouse arrives."

Chapter Forty-seven
no choice

DESPEREAUX STOOD TREMBLING
on the steps. The thread was most definitely gone.
He could not hear it. He could not see it. He should
have tied it to himself when he had the chance. But
it was too late now.

Despereaux's dire situation suddenly became
quite clear to him. He was a two-ounce mouse
alone in a dark, twisting dungeon full of rats. He
had nothing but a sewing needle with which to
defend himself. He had to find a princess. And he
had to save her once he found her.

"It's impossible," he said to the darkness. "I can't do it."

He stood very still. "I'll go back," he said. But he didn't move. "I have to go back." He took a step backwards. "But I can't go back. I don't have a choice. I have no choice."

He took one step forward. And then another.

"No choice," his heart beat out to him as he went down the stairs, "no choice, no choice, no choice."

At the bottom of the stairs, the rat Botticelli sat waiting, and when Despereaux stepped from the last stair onto the dungeon floor Botticelli called out to him as if he were a long-lost friend. "Ah," said Botticelli, "there you are. Exactly. I've been waiting for you."

Despereaux saw the dark shape of a rat, that thing that he had feared and dreaded for so long, finally step out of the gloom and come to greet him.

"Welcome, welcome," said Botticelli.

Despereaux put his paw on the needle.

"Ah," said Botticelli, "you are armed. How charming." He put his paws up in the air. "I surrender. Oh, yes, certainly, exactly, I surrender!"

"I…" said Despereaux.

"Yes," said Botticelli. "You." He took *the* locket from around his neck. He began to swing it back and forth. "Please, go on."

"I don't want to hurt you," said Despereaux. "I just need to get by you. I … I am on a quest."

"Really?" said Botticelli. "How extraordinary. A mouse on a quest." Back and forth, back and forth went the locket. "A quest for what?"

"A quest to save the princess."

"The princess," said Botticelli, "the princess, the princess. Everything seems to be about the princess these days. The king's men were down here searching for her, you know. They didn't find her. That goes without saying. But now a mouse has arrived. And he is on a quest to save the princess."

"Yes," said Despereaux. He took a step to the left of Botticelli.

"How inspiring," said Botticelli. He lazily took a step to his right, blocking Despereaux's way. "Why the hurry, little friend?"

"Because," said Despereaux, "I have to —"

"Yes. Yes. You have to save the princess. Exactly. But before you save her, you must find her. Correct?"

"Yes," said Despereaux.

"What if," said Botticelli, "what if I told you that I know exactly where the princess is? What if I told you that I could take you right directly to her?"

"Ummm," said Despereaux. His voice shook. His paw on the needle trembled. "Why would you do that?"

"Why would I do that? Why would I help you? Why … to be of service. To do my part for humanity. To aid in the rescue of a princess."

"But you are a…"

"A rat," supplied Botticelli. "Yes. I am a rat. And I see by your trem-trem-trembling that the greatly exaggerated rumours of our evil nature have reached your oversized ears."

"Yes," said Despereaux.

"If," said Botticelli, swinging the locket back and forth, "if you allow me to be of assistance, you will be doing me a tremendous favour. Not only can I do a good deed for you and for the princess, but my actions will help to dispel this terrible myth of evil that seems to surround rats everywhere. Will you let me assist you? Will you let me assist myself and my kind?"

Reader, was it a trick?

Of course it was!

Botticelli did not want to be of service. Far from it. You know what Botticelli wanted. He wanted others to suffer. Specifically, he wanted this small mouse to suffer. How best to do that?

Why, take him right directly to what he wanted. The princess. Let him see what his heart desired, and then, and only then, faced with what he loved, would Despereaux die. And at the end of it all, how tasty the mouse would be ... seasoned with hope and tears and flour and oil and thwarted love!

"My name, little friend, is Botticelli Remorso. And you may trust me. You must trust me. Will you tell me your name?"

"Despereaux. Despereaux Tilling."

"Despereaux Tilling, take your paw from your weapon. Come with me."

Despereaux stared at him.

"Come, come," said Botticelli, "let go of your

needle. Take hold of my tail. I will lead you to your princess. I promise."

What, reader, in your experience, is the promise of a rat worth?

That's right.

Zero. Zip. Nil. Absolutely nothing.

But I must ask you this question too. What else was there for Despereaux to hold onto?

You are right again.

Nothing.

And so the mouse reached out. He took hold of the rat's tail.

Chapter Forty-eight ✑
on the tail of a rat

HAVE YOU EVER had hold of the tail of a rat? At best it is an unpleasant sensation, scaly and cold, similar to holding onto a small, narrow snake. At worst, when you are dependent upon a rat for your survival, and when a part of you is certain that you are being led nowhere except to your death, it is a hideous sensation, indeed, to have nothing but a rat's tail to cling to.

Nonetheless, Despereaux held onto Botticelli Remorso. And the rat led him deeper and deeper into the dungeon.

Despereaux's eyes had, by this point, adjusted

quite well to the darkness, though it would have been better if they had not, for the things he saw made him shiver and shake.

What did he see?

He saw that the floor of the dungeon was littered with tufts of fur, knots of red thread and the skeletons of mice. Everywhere there were tiny white bones glowing in the darkness. And he saw, in the dungeon tunnels through which Botticelli led him, the bones of human beings too, grinning skulls and delicate finger bones, rising up out of the darkness and pointing towards some truth best left unspoken.

Despereaux closed his eyes.

But it didn't help. He saw as if his eyes were still open wide the bones, the tufts of hair, the knots of thread, the despair.

"Ha-ha, exactly!" Botticelli laughed as he negotiated the twists and turns. "Oh, yes, exactly."

If what was in front of Despereaux was too horrible to contemplate, what followed behind him was, perhaps, even worse: rats, a happy, hungry, vengeful parade of rats, their noses up in the air, sniffing, sniffing.

Despereaux closed his eyes.

"Mouse!" sang out one rat joyfully.

"Yes, oh yes, mouse," agreed another. "But something else, too."

"Soup!" called out another rat.

"Yes, soup," the others agreed.

"Blood!" sang a rat.

"Blood," they all agreed together.

And then they sang: "Here, mousie, mousie, mousie! Here, little mousie!"

Botticelli called out to the other rats. "Mine," he said. "This little treasure is all mine, gentlemen and ladies. Please, I beg you. Do not infringe on my discovery."

"Mr Remorso," said Despereaux. He turned and looked behind him and saw the rats, their red eyes and their smiling mouths. He closed his eyes again. He kept them closed. "Mr Remorso!" he shouted.

"Yes?" said Botticelli.

"Mr Remorso," said Despereaux. And he was crying now. He couldn't help it. "Please. The princess."

"Tears!" shouted the rats. "We smell tears, mousie, we do."

"Please!" shouted Despereaux.

"Little friend," said Botticelli. "Little Despereaux Tilling. I promised you. And I will keep that promise."

The rat stopped.

"Look ahead of you," he said. "What do you see?"

Despereaux opened his eyes.

"Light," he said.

"Exactly," said Botticelli. "Light."

Chapter Forty-nine
what do you want, Miggery Sow?!

AGAIN, READER, we must go backwards, before we go forwards. We must consider, for a moment, what had occurred with the rat and the serving girl and the princess down in the dungeon before Despereaux made his way to them.

What happened was this: Roscuro led the Pea and Mig deep into the dungeon to a hidden chamber, and there he directed Mig to put the princess in chains.

"Gor," said Mig, "she's going to have a hard time learning her lessons if she's all chained up like."

"Do as I say," said Roscuro.

"Maybe," said Mig, "before I lock her up, her and me could switch outfits, so we could start in already with her being me and me being a princess."

"Oh, yes," said Roscuro. "Certainly. A wonderful idea, Miss Miggery. Princess, take off your crown and give it to the serving girl."

The Pea sighed and took off her crown and handed it to Mig, and Mig put it on and it slid immediately right down her small head and came to rest, quite painfully, on her poor, abused ears. "It's a biggish thing," she said, "and painful-like."

"Well, well," said Roscuro.

"How do I look?" Mig asked, smiling at him.

"Ridiculous," he said. "Laughable."

Mig stood, blinking back tears. "You mean I don't look like a princess?" she said to the rat.

"I mean," said Roscuro, "you will *never* look like a princess, no matter how big a crown you put on your tiny head. You look exactly like the fool you are and always will be. Now, make yourself useful and chain the princess up. Dress-up time is over."

Mig sniffed and wiped at her eyes and then bent to look at the pile of chains and locks on the floor.

"And now, Princess," he said, "I'm afraid that the time for *your* truth has arrived. I will now tell you what your future holds. As you consigned me to darkness, so I consign you, too, to a life spent in this dungeon."

Mig looked up. "Ain't she going upstairs to be a serving maid?"

"No," said Roscuro.

"Ain't I going to be a princess, then?"

"No," said Roscuro.

"But I want to be a princess."

"No one," said Roscuro, "cares what you want."

As you know, reader, Miggery Sow had heard this sentiment expressed many times in her short life. But now, in the dungeon, it hit her full force: The rat was right. No one cared what she wanted. No one had ever cared. And perhaps, worst of all, no one ever would care.

"I want…!" cried Mig.

"Shhhh," said the princess.

"Shut up," said the rat.

"I want…" sobbed Mig, "I want … I want…"

"What do you want, Mig?" the princess said softly.

"Eh?" shouted Mig.

"What do you want, Miggery Sow?!" the princess shouted.

"Don't ask her that," said Roscuro. "Shut up. Shut up."

But it was too late. The words had been said; the question, at last, had been asked. The world stopped spinning and all of creation held its breath, waiting to hear what it was that Miggery Sow wanted.

"I want..." said Mig.

"Yes?" shouted the Pea.

"I want my ma!" cried Mig, into the silent, waiting world. *"I want my ma!"*

"Oh," said the princess. She held out her hand to Mig.

Mig took hold of it.

"I want my mother, too," said the princess softly. And she squeezed Mig's hand.

"Stop it!" shouted Roscuro. "Chain her up. Chain her up."

"Gor," said Mig, "I ain't going to do it. You can't make me do it. *I* got the knife, don't I?" She took the knife and held it up.

"What do you want, Miggery Sow?!"

"If you have any sense at all," said Roscuro, "and I heartily doubt that you do, you will not use that instrument on me. Without me you will never find your way out of the dungeon, and you will starve to death here, or worse."

"Gor," said Mig, "then lead us out now, or I will chop you up into little rat bits."

"No," said Roscuro. "The princess will stay here in the darkness. And you, Mig, will stay with her."

"But I want to go upstairs," said Mig.

"I'm afraid that we are stuck here, Mig," said the princess, "unless the rat has a change of heart and decides to lead us out."

"There will be no changes of heart," said Roscuro. "None."

"Gor," said Mig. She lowered the knife.

And so the rat and the princess and the serving girl sat together in the dungeon as, outside the castle, the sun rose and moved through the sky and sank to the earth again, and night fell. They sat together until the candle had burned out and another one had to be lit. They sat together in the dungeon. They sat. And sat.

And, reader, truthfully, they might be sitting there still if a mouse had not arrived.

Chapter Fifty
in which the princess says his name

"PRINCESS!" Despereaux shouted. "Princess, I have come to save you."

The Princess Pea heard her name. She looked up.

"Despereaux," she whispered.

And then she shouted it, "Despereaux!"

Reader, nothing is sweeter in this sad world than the sound of someone you love calling your name.

Nothing.

For Despereaux, the sound was worth everything: his lost tail, his trip to the dungeon and back out of it and back into it again.

He ran towards the princess.

But Roscuro, baring his teeth, blocked the mouse's way.

The princess cried, "Oh no, rat, please. Don't hurt him. He is my friend."

Mig said, "Don't worry, Princess. I will save the meecy."

She took the kitchen knife. She aimed to cut off the rat's head, but she missed her mark.

"Whoopsie," said Miggery Sow.

Chapter Fifty-one
what is that smell?

"OWWWWWWWW!" screamed Roscuro.

He turned to look at where his tail had been, and as he did so, Despereaux drew his needle and placed the sharp tip of it right where the rat's heart should be.

"Don't move," said Despereaux. "I will kill you."

"Ha-ha-ha!" Botticelli laughed from the sidelines. "Exactly." He slapped his tail on the floor in approval. "Absolutely delightful. A mouse is going to kill a rat. Oh, all of this is much better than I had anticipated. I love it when mice come to the dungeon."

"Don't move," said Despereaux. "I will kill you."

"Let me see!" said the other rats, pushing and shoving.

"Stand back," Botticelli told them, still laughing. "Let the mouse do his work."

Despereaux held the trembling needle against Roscuro's heart. The mouse knew that as a knight it was his duty to protect the princess. But would killing the rat really make the darkness go away?

Despereaux bowed his head ever so slightly. And as he did so, his whiskers brushed against the rat's nose.

Roscuro sniffed.

"What ... is that smell?" he asked.

"Mousie blood!" shouted one rat.

"Blood and bones!" shouted another.

"You're smelling tears," said Botticelli. "Tears and thwarted love."

"Exactly," said Roscuro. "And yet ... there's something else."

He sniffed again.

And the smell of soup crashed through his soul like a great wave, bringing with it the memory of light, the chandelier, the music, the laughter, everything, all the things that were not, would never, could never be available to him as a rat.

"*Soup*," moaned Roscuro.

And he began to cry.

"Booooooo!" shouted Botticelli.

"*Sssssssss*," hissed the other rats.

"Kill me," said Roscuro. He fell down before Despereaux. "It will never work. All I wanted was some light. That is why I brought the princess here, really, just for some beauty ... some light of my own."

"Please," shouted Botticelli, "do kill him! He is a miserable excuse for a rat."

"No, Despereaux," said the princess. "Don't kill him."

Despereaux lowered his needle. He turned and looked at the Pea.

"Boooo!" shouted Botticelli again. "Kill him! Kill him. All this goodness is making me sick. I've lost my appetite."

"Gor!" shouted Mig, waving her knife. "I'll kill him."

"No, wait," said the princess. "Roscuro," she said to the rat.

"What?" he said. Tears were falling out of his eyes and creeping down his whiskers and dripping onto the dungeon floor.

And then the princess took a deep breath and put a hand on her heart.

I think, reader, that she was feeling the same thing that Despereaux had felt when he was faced with his father begging him for forgiveness. That is, Pea was aware suddenly of how fragile her heart was, how much darkness was inside it, fighting, always, with the light. She did not like the rat. She would never like the rat, but she knew what she must do to save her own heart.

And so here are the words that the princess spoke to her enemy.

She said, "Roscuro, would you like some soup?"

The rat sniffed. "Don't torment me," he said.

"I promise you," said the princess, "that if you lead us out of here, I will get Cook to make you some soup. And you can eat it in the banquet hall."

"Speaking of eating," shouted one of the rats, "give us the mousie!"

"Yeah," shouted another, "hand over the mouse!"

"Who would want him now?" said Botticelli. "The flavour of him will be ruined. All that forgiveness and goodness. Yuk. I, for one, am leaving."

"Soup in the banquet hall?" Roscuro asked the princess.

"Yes," said the Pea.

"Really?"

"Truly. I promise."

"Gor!" shouted Mig. "Soup is illegal."

"But soup is good," said Despereaux.

"Yes," said the Pea. "Isn't it?"

The princess bent down before the mouse. "You are my knight," she said to him, "with a shining needle. And I am so glad that you found me. Let's go upstairs. Let's eat some soup."

And, reader, they did.

Chapter Fifty-two
happily ever after

BUT THE QUESTION you want answered, I know, is did they live happily ever after?

Yes ... and no.

What of Roscuro? Did he live happily ever after? Well ... the Princess Pea gave him free access to the upstairs of the castle. And he was allowed to go back and forth from the darkness of the dungeon to the light of the upstairs. But, alas, he never really belonged in either place: the sad fate, I am afraid, of those whose hearts break and then mend in crooked ways. But the rat, in seeking forgiveness, did manage to shed some small light, some happiness, into another life.

How?

Roscuro, reader, told the princess about the prisoner who had once owned a red tablecloth, and the princess saw to it that the prisoner was released. And Roscuro led the man up out of the dungeon and to his daughter, Miggery Sow. Mig, as you might have guessed, did not get to be a princess. But her father, to atone for what he had done, treated her like one for the rest of his days.

And what of Despereaux? Did he live happily ever after? Well, he did not marry the princess, if that is what you mean by happily ever after. Even in a world as strange as this one a mouse and a princess cannot marry.

But, reader, they can be friends.

And they were. Together, they had many adventures. Those adventures, however, are another story, and this story, I'm afraid, must now draw to a close.

But before you leave, reader, imagine this: Imagine an adoring king and a glowing princess, a serving girl with a crown on her head and a rat with a spoon on his, all gathered around a table in a banquet hall.

In the middle of the table, there is a great kettle of soup. Sitting in the place of honour, right next to the princess, is a very small mouse with big ears.

And peeking out from behind a dusty velvet curtain, looking in amazement at the scene before them, are four other mice.

"*Mon Dieu*, look, look," says Antoinette. "He lives. He lives! And he seems such the happy mouse."

"Forgiven," whispers Lester.

"Cripes," says Furlough, "unbelievable."

"Just so," says the thread-master Hovis, smiling, "just so."

And, reader, it is just so.

Isn't it?

THE END

Coda

Do you remember when Despereaux was in the dungeon, cupped in Gregory the jailer's hand, whispering a story in the old man's ear?

I would like it very much if you thought of me as a mouse telling you a story, this story, with the whole of my heart, whispering it in your ear in order to save myself from the darkness, and to save you from the darkness, too.

"Stories are light," Gregory the jailer told Despereaux.

Reader, I hope you have found some light here.

Acknowledgements

*I am grateful to the following individuals for their
unflagging love, patience and support during the
telling of the mouse's tale: Karla Rydrych, Jane St
Anthony, Cindy Rogers, Jane Resh Thomas, Jason
William Walton, Alison McGhee, Holly McGhee,
Lisa Beck and Tracey Bailey. Despereaux and I
are also deeply indebted to Kara LaReau –
editor, visionary, friend.*

*This book was written with the help of a generous
grant from the McKnight Foundation.*